Braddock's Gold

Jay Heavner

Publisher Page
an imprint of Headline Books, Inc.
Terra Alta, WV

Braddock's Gold

Jay Heavner

copyright ©2015 Jay Heavner

To order additional copies of this book or for book publishing information, or to contact the author:

Headline Books, Inc.
P.O. Box 52
Terra Alta, WV 26764
www.PublisherPage.com
800-570-5951

Publisher Page is an imprint of Headline Books

ISBN 13: 9781882658145

Library of Congress Control Number: 2014948922

PRINTED IN THE UNITED STATES OF AMERICA

*I would like to dedicate the book to my wife's
and my parents, Orval and Bessie Kenney
and G.Edward and Frances Heavner.*

Acknowledgments

I would like to thank my wife, Vivian, and all my family for their patience while their crazy husband and father was absorbed in writing this book. Thanks to those who encouraged me in this endeavor, Mary Lou Wagoner, Tim Mace, all my friends at the Plant St. Lucie Nuclear Power Station, Judy and Verne Haskell, friends at church, and my extended family. I know others too I am forgetting to list. You know who you are. Thanks so much. :) And to Cathy Teets for taking a chance on this story.

Chapter 1

The sun rose just past 6:00 a.m. over the small town of Fort Ashby, West Virginia that Friday before Memorial Day weekend in 1995. Tomorrow, throngs of people would leave the big cities of Washington, D.C. and Baltimore, Maryland—a three hour drive due east of the little community—seeking recreation over the long weekend. Some would even find their way to the nearby South Branch of the Potomac and other streams that fed the larger Potomac River as did Patterson Creek.

Little Timmy Miltenberger woke early. It was the first day off from school for the summer. He would be in the fourth grade when school started in the fall. Today, he wanted to ride his bike down the dirt road and play in the afternoon, but first he wanted to do some fishing. His big brother, Robby, aged 16, was supposed to be watching Little Timmy.

Mom and Dad would be at their jobs. Timmy had been a shock to his Mom and Dad. It had been eight years since there had been a new child in the home. After five children, the Miltenbergers, good Catholics, thought they had enough, but surprise, surprise! Mary found herself pregnant with a menopause baby. They loved all their kids and this one, although not planned, would be no diffcrent. She and husband Joseph believed all children were gifts from God. They laughed how God put them together, yes, Mary and Joseph. The family joke had been they would name their first born, Jesus. They did in a way, Joshua; the Hebrew-English version of Jesus became the elder's name. Timmy and Robby were the only two still at home, the other siblings were grown and off making their own lives. It hadn't been an easy pregnancy for Mary, now an older woman. Tim was born early, a preemie and small, which had led to his nickname, Little Tim, as many people knew him. The doctor said given time, he would catch up, but for now he was one of the smaller kids in his class of 30.

It was about 7:00 a.m. when he got out of bed, not that Timmy cared, or for that matter could yet tell time. He quickly dressed, no hand-me downs for him. The other siblings had those, but he got new clothes, having no one close for hand-me downs. Into the kitchen he went, got a bowl of corn flakes, poured in some milk, and ate it quickly. He grabbed a banana for a snack, went out the door, and stood on the porch. There, about 40 feet away and down a moderate hill was his delight, Patterson Creek, or just "the crick" as it was known locally. The old house had been there a long time, seen many floods, and had water one foot deep in it back in the 1960s. Then came the great flood of 1985. That one broke all-time records on many streams in the area. Fortunately, for the Miltenbergers back in 1981, their insurance company had required for them to have continued coverage, they must raise their home. The house must be elevated eighteen inches per new government regulations mandated for homes in flood plains.

The national malaise of the last four years was slowly lifting and new hope was stirring. The hostages in Iran had been released and a new president had been elected. With him came tax cuts and new regulations like the ones that required the house to be raised. It would take two additional years for the changed economic policies to kick in fully and by that point the economy had improved significantly. But this was 1981 and times were still hard. Mr. Miltenberger contacted several companies for prices. He settled on the contractor that offered to raise the house an additional six inches over the new government requirements for no additional cost and it was a good price, too. Regulations could change again he said. This would also move the house to the so called thousand-year flood level and give more insurance savings. Only once every thousand years was a flood expected at this new level. Joe was glad he did. The flood of 1985 crested a mere two inches below the floor. The pink fiberglass insulation in the floor joists was ruined, but otherwise, the house was unharmed. He replaced it before winter and considered himself lucky compared to what many others in the area suffered, but little Timmy knew none of this. He was born several years afterward and in his lifetime the creek had behaved itself and remained within its banks… mostly. Last fall, when the water got too high, the family left for higher ground with relatives, but the water only threatened, never getting in the house.

He went over to the shed and opened the wooden box full of decaying leaves, dark soil, and night crawlers for fishing. They went in an old can with some of the moist dirt. He stuck the banana in his hip pocket, grabbed his pole, and headed for the creek. It was warm enough for swimming now, but Momma had forbidden it unless someone was there with Timmy and he listened this time. The creek was milky today. His daddy would have said something about it raining upstream, but here it had been a little dry. He noted some shoe prints in the mud along the creek bank. They were quite large. He wondered who had made them this early in the morning. *Probably that strange old man, Dan Phares, who lived on the neighboring farm*, he thought to himself. He had been scared of him the first time he saw him. His dad assured him Ole Dan was harmless, though he looked frightening. His dad said Dan had a disability. Little Tim was not sure what a "disability" was, but he knew he did not want one. Dad also told him he could not catch Dan's disability and that made him feel better. He had seen Ole Dan walking along the creek several times since then and had spoken to him. Ole Dan seemed a lot smarter than he looked and also a good guy once you got past his weird looks.

Timmy baited his hook with the night crawler and threw it in the water. *Good cast*, he thought. He liked to go out at night with his flashlight, usually after a rain and catch worms. Find one with the light, walk slowly closer, and grab the part that stuck out of the ground. Don't pull too hard, or you will break it. Hold on, wait for the worm to tire and then slowly pull it out of the dark soil by the creek.

By 9:00, he had a stringer of sunfish, sunnys as he called them, one small bass, and an unknown. Known or not, Momma would fry them up for him. It was time to quit so he reeled the fishing line in. Oh great, he'd snagged something. Old tires, shoes, and assorted trash he had caught before. With a little jerk, the line came free and he reeled whatever it was through the cloudy water. To his surprise, he had a small muddy cloth at the end of his line. Why, it was a little bag with drawstrings and heavy, too. He emptied the contents in his hand, coins. One, two, three, a total of ten quarters. Right size, but they were the wrong color, yellow. *Must be those Indian dollars his first grade teacher, Mrs. Wilmot, had shown his class.* She had it in her hand in the front of the room and Timmy sat halfway back so he didn't get too good a look. One year, she had passed coins around and some had gone missing. She did not make that mistake again. Ten coins, ten heavy coins. Well, he knew what he would do with one of them tomorrow being Sunday. And another he would cut up with a hack saw for fishing line sinkers. He could get six or eight pieces from it. That would be cheaper than buying and he had this to use already. *Got to clean the fish and then hide my new found wealth away in my room,* he thought. It had been a good day so far for Timmy. He would wear himself out playing and riding his bike and need a nap later.

"Hey, where you been?" It was his big brother Robby who was supposed to be watching him.

"Right here, just got done fishin'," and Timmy held out his catch.

"Looks good. Stay out of trouble." With that the older brother turned and went back into the house.

Yup, thought Timmy, *looks like it's gonna be a good summer though nothin' excitin' ever happens 'round here.*

Chapter 2

Tom rolled over in his bed and looked at the clock, 4:00 a.m. Why, it just seemed only half hour ago it had said 3:59. Time was moving at a snail's pace tonight. This was about the fifth time he had woken from a restless sleep. He knew there was no point in trying to go back to sleep. He couldn't. Carefully, he slid out of the bed so his wife wouldn't wake up. He had kept her up with his tossing and turning and now he just wanted her to get some restful, refreshing sleep. He dressed in jeans and WVU t-shirt, and headed quietly into the kitchen. Tom put the coffee on to perk. Love that Chock Full o' Nuts brand. Not only was it great coffee, but the company founder, William Black, had also established the Parkinson's Disease Foundation. Tom's late father had that dreaded disease. Tom was always thankful for people who were blessed with money used it to help humanity. So many were like Scrooge and hoarded their wealth. He grabbed a bowl, some granola and milk, and attempted to eat. His appetite was lacking. *Finally, the coffee's done*, he thought. He poured a cup and sipped, *ah, good to the last drop*. He loved the flavor. Tom took the half-finished bowl of cereal and put it and the man-sized spoon in the sink. Finding a large piece of paper, he wrote a note, "Honey, couldn't sleep. You know why. Off to the usual place. Be home ...... Tom."

He walked out of the house, being careful not to slam the door, and opened the door to his pickup truck. *Good old faithful truck*, he thought, *181,000 miles and still going strong. Should be able to get 300,000 out of her if the rust from the winter road salt didn't get her first.* He started her up and, barely touching the gas, quietly eased her down the driveway to WV Route 28, Bloody 28. The crooked, winding road had claimed numerous lives and maimed many others. The local people had gone to the state capital in Charleston to try to get the state to improve the road. Little had been done. Lack of funds they always said. Tom suspected there was more than that as to why so little had been done. And now as the area's population grew, the problem was getting worse and worse. There were so many people trying to escape the taxes of neighboring Maryland. He eased the car onto the highway and headed toward the sleepy little community of Short Gap. He saw a car still parked at a local watering hole. *Probably a drunk sleeping it off. Better he did that than try to drive home*. Passing Rt. 956 the road turned south and followed the small stream called Turners Run toward Fort Ashby. Somewhere along the stream in the mid 1700s, Colonial soldiers had skirmished with a small band of French troops and their Indian allies when this area was still the American frontier.

The moonlight reflected off the mist along the valley floor. For a moment, Tom was back in the Ia Drang valley in Vietnam on that horrible day that changed his life forever. The truck's rear wheel drifted onto the dirt shoulder. This woke Tom from his terrible dreamlike state. He pulled the truck back onto the asphalt, but it fishtailed slightly as he did. On he went, past the closed up Sunoco station with the huge flag painted on the block front, then by the Catholic Church. A light was on in the priest's quarters. *Looks like Father Frank was up early. Must be going somewhere*. Monday was his day off and he usually slept in unless he had something special going on. Tom slowed the truck as he neared Siple's Turn, site of many accidents over the years. He knew of mothers who still warned their adult children to be careful on the turn, even the ones who had been around it hundreds—if not thousands of times. His headlights pierced the darkness the streetlights of Fort Ashby hadn't chased away. Over Patterson Creek on the new bridge to the one traffic light in the town, wait for a car before turning left, probably someone heading to work and down Dans Run Road past the volunteer fire department, the Methodist Church, and the old school building that had seen many uses over the years and now served as the Community Center. Tom's small congregation met there on Sunday. He was the Pastor. He hit the turn signal, though there was no one on the road to see it, slowed, turned at the old fort, Ashby's Fort, from which the town got its name. Then he drove up the one lane paved road to where it got steep. There he gave it some gas, climbed the hill, got to the top, turned right, pulled the truck onto the gravel, and turned off the engine. *So quiet. So dark. So still.* Slowly, his eyes adjusted to the dark. The sun would be coming up soon. It came up early at this latitude in midsummer. He could already see a hint of light in the east behind the hill. A dog barked somewhere in town followed by another answering. There was no breeze; another hot one today. Summer had arrived early this year. And then in the dark his mind focused on why he had come here today, to the Fort Ashby Cemetery. This was the fifth anniversary of his son's death, Brian, his eldest son. He had taken a gun and shot himself in the head. He had done this a year to the day Sarah, Tom's first wife and Brian's mother, had been killed by a drunk driver on Bloody WV Route 28. She was the one that could always reach Brian through the madness. And then, as he had done, oh so many times in his old truck, Tom broke down and wept.

Chapter 3

Tap, tap. Tap, tap, tap.

Tap, tap, tap. Tap, tap, tap. There it was again. Tom slowly awakened, and looked around. *Where was he?* Then he remembered. He'd done it again; fell asleep on the bench seat in his truck.

Tap, tap, tap. He looked at where the sound was coming from and saw a familiar face.

"Hey, Tom, wake up!" the female voice said.

Tom sat up, rolled the window down, and spoke to the voice, "Hello, Jenny. Looks like I done it again." Tom remembered the first time he met Jenny. It had not been too pleasant. She found him asleep in his truck when she came in to work. She was the caretaker of the cemetery. She thought he was a drunk sleeping it off and didn't care to get too close, so she called the cops. It had been the Sheriff who woke him that day, Sheriff Wagoner of Mineral County. One thing about living in a small town, everyone knows everyone, well mostly. Sometimes that's good; sometimes it's not.

That day it was good. Tom had gone to school with Donnie Wagoner. Tom remembered that morning well. "What the Sam Hill are you doin' here?" Donnie had woken him with a start.

Embarrassed, Tom explained how he hadn't been able to sleep, and had come up here to where his son was buried. He still grieved for his son and wife. They walked over to the little office, had coffee, and talked. People in small towns still have time to listen to each other. That's how he met Jenny. And now today, just as she'd done a number of times, she had tapped on his window.

"Beautiful day, still got that morning coolness to it," Tom said to her.

"Yes, a good morning to you. Still missing your family?" she asked.

Tom nodded, "Don't know if I'll ever get over it, Jenny."

"Yah, I know, Mom's been gone about ten years now, and I still miss her. Sometimes I go over to her grave over there and have a little talk with her. It's kind of one sided, but it still makes me feel better," Jenny responded sympathetically. "I see a lot of regulars come up here and do the same. Oh, your wife called, said you'd be here. Seems the Padre wants to have breakfast with you over at Cindy's. You better get moving."

Tom looked at his watch, just past 8:00. *Good, Father Frank wouldn't have been waiting too long.*

"Thanks, Jenny, I'll be going. Till next time?" Tom answered.

She smiled and waved as he drove off to Cindy's Restaurant, just a short drive away. He kept to the twenty-five mph speed limit and thought of events since his son's death. *Undiagnosed schizophrenia, how many more were out there? How had everyone missed it? It all seemed so clear now.* Tom had taken classes with NAMI, National Association for Mental Illness. It was hard for him to believe that it often takes ten years to get the right diagnosis from the professionals. His son had always been difficult as a teen. ADD, ADHD they said. *Why was it so hard to see what was wrong and get treatment?* Still, from what he learned from the classes, it was a wonder any of us was walking around upright. Billions and billions of cells in the brain, each with up to fifty connections to each other, and they all had to be working right. *Amazing the creative design behind all this,* Tom mused to himself as he drove.

He turned off North Street, better known as Dan's Run Road, behind the Dairy Dip, and into a parking spot there on the old town square. George Washington had been through this area many times back in colonial times. The first time was as a surveyor at age sixteen. Years later, as commander of Colonial forces, he commissioned the old Fort to be built for protection of the settlers from the French and Indians when this was the wild frontier. The last was on his way to stop the Whiskey Rebellion. This town had a lot of history, but now it was time to see what Father Frank wanted and feed his growling stomach.

Chapter 4

Tom climbed out of his truck and headed toward the front double door to Cindy's Restaurant. He saw a couple he had gone to high school with coming out, greeted them, wanted to talk but knowing Father Frank was waiting, cut it short and went in. Near the cash register by the door, he saw the sticky buns. He had a weakness for them, but wasn't hungry for them today. He looked around the place and saw the Padre waving for him from a booth. Tom walked over, stuck out his hand, but before he could move, Father Frank was up from his seat and gave the surprised Tom a hug. He let go and from a smile as broad as his face said, "So good to see you, brother."

That Father Frank, what a character. He always seemed to know what a person needed, Tom thought. Now feeling embarrassed and a little red in the face, Tom smiled and said "So good to see you too, brother."

They had no more than sat down in the booth, than Carol, the waitress, was there with coffee. "Coffee?" she asked with a big grin on her face. She had been watching the whole time as had been most of the patrons there. This was usually a fun place to work, and you never knew what kind of cut up horseplay would occur that day.

"I'll have some, Carol," Tom said.

"Black as usual, Tom?" He returned the grin.

"Yes, please."

"And you Padre?" Carol asked still grinning now almost giggling.

"Give me a warmer up, okay? I've had enough to float a battleship already," he said.

"Okay."

She poured the coffee and asked Tom, "Anything else for you?"

"I think I'd like a number one." Before she could ask, Tom added, "Make it wheat bread for the toast, and a tab of honey to sweeten me up."

Still grinning she responded, "Coming right up and Tom, you're so sweet, I don't know why you don't have bees flying around you. I don't know how you wife stands you."

With that she left and headed for the kitchen with the order. Tom looked at the Padre and asked, "Well, how ya doin'?"

"Pretty good, God is good. Even a bad day is good with Him," answered Father Frank.

"And you? You look like you slept in a truck," he commented.

"I did."

"Oh, another one of those nights?"

"Yah, another one of those nights," Tom groaned. "It's been five years today since his death and six since Sarah's."

Father Frank knew all about the son's death. He had stopped in at Tom's house a few days after the funeral to wish him condolences. They had a long chat and had been close friends since then. Tom was a lay pastor for his church, and Father Frank knew how men of the cloth often hold the grief in and are isolated because of this. The Padre was really a people person.

They first met after the incident at the church shortly after Father Frank had been assigned there. Someone spray painted vulgarities, swastikas, and racial epithets on the outside of the church. Tom had talked to him at the church and asked him not to judge the town by the actions of one or a few. While there had been trouble in the past, nowadays most people could see beyond the color of a man's skin. Father Frank was black, as black as the ace of spades. A black priest for an all-white congregation. It was true that a few people had left, but the church was growing handily. And most of those that left had returned.

"Oh, in all the excitement, I forgot what I needed to do," Tom said.

"And what's that?" the Padre looked at him.

"I got to pee. My eyes are turning yellow." With that Tom got out of the booth and headed for the bathroom. The Padre just shook his head and smiled.

Chapter 5

When Tom got back from the rest room, his breakfast was waiting for him at the booth. As he sat down, he said to Father Frank, "Wow that was fast."

"You're so predictable. I think the cook started it when you walked through the door. That and you took a long time in there."

"Just takin' care of business," Tom chirped. "Now what was it you wanted to see me about? I'll listen while I eat this food."

"I blessed it while you were busy. Yes, eat, and I'll tell you what's on my mind."

Tom stuffed some home fries in his mouth and then took a sip of coffee.

"Ever seen one of these?" With that, he pulled out a coin, golden in color, somewhat bigger than a quarter and laid it next to the plate near Tom's easy-over eggs.

"No, don't think so. What is it?" Tom asked.

"Look closer, and think for a minute," the Padre requested.

Tom picked it up. It was heavy for its size. *Where had he seen something like this before? Where indeed?* Tom laid it down on the table and said, "Okay, I give up. What is it?"

Tom reached for his coffee and took a big sip.

Father Frank looked at him seriously. "It's an English guinea. It contains about 3 ounces of gold."

Tom almost choked on his coffee. "Did you say three ounces of gold?!"

Father Frank nodded.

"Do you know what that worth!?"

Father Frank nodded again. "Yes, I know what an ounce of gold is going for today."

"That's a lot of money. Where did you get that thing?" Tom asked.

"Keep this in confidence please. It showed up in the offering at the church two Sundays ago," he said lowering his voice. "Took me this long to find out what it was and how it got there."

Tom nodded knowingly. "Keep talking. I'm all ears."

Father Frank began the tale. "Finding out what it was turned out not to be too difficult. I went over to the library and got a book on old coins, American and British. That fellow on the front is King George II of England. That coin was made in the mid-1700s."

Then it dawned on Tom where he'd seen something like that before, at the museum at the old fort, Fort Ashby. "I think I may know where it came from," Tom interrupted. "This whole area around here has a lot of colonial history. Settlement began back in the early 1700s." It was probably lost by someone back there and just got found by...."

The Padre cut him off. "I wondered about that, too, but listen to this. I took it into a coin shop in Cumberland to have it looked at. The owner's eyes 'bout fell out of their sockets when he saw the coin. He offered a thousand dollars right there on the spot. I told him it was not for sale. Then he started on this tale about Braddock's Gold. Ever hear about it?"

"Braddock's Gold," Tom thought aloud. "Yah, there's an old legend, more of an old wife's tale about General Braddock of French and Indian War fame or infamy depending on who you talk to. They buried the troop's payroll in gold somewhere up on the Youghiogheny River in Pennsylvania. The British troops that knew its location were all killed along with General Braddock in the Battle of the Monongehela near present-day Pittsburgh. The gold was never recovered and disappeared into the sands of history."

Father Frank looked at him knowingly. "Well, not quite. According to the coin dealer, a few coins have been turning up every now and then beginning at the start of the American Revolution, maybe even a little sooner."

"Wow. That's quite a story. How did you get the coin?" Tom inquired.

"I'd rather tell you that in my office at the church. Finish your breakfast. You haven't taken a bite in five minutes, bet those eggs are getting cold," the Padre answered. "Hey, Carol, could you get us some more coffee, please?" And then he looked sternly at Tom. "No more on this till you are done."

What could Tom say? Padre knows best. The rest of this story would have to wait till breakfast was finished. Tom ate fast.

Chapter 6

Alan Grey sat on the porch of the old hard-scrapple farmhouse in an ancient rocking chair. The house in the big meadow sat high on the hill and faced the east. Alan sat there many a morning sipping on a cup of coffee and enjoying the solitude. The house was far from the country lane that served as the main road into this isolated area. Trees blocked the view of the road. The only way you knew there was traffic passing by was a little auto noise or maybe a little dust from the road shoulders when it was very dry, like now. The angled ridge it was built on ended in a high cliff. The other side of the ridge was extremely steep with lots of boulders sticking out. There was only one practical way to get to the old house, up the long farm lane that led from the main road. At that point there was a metal gate with a sturdy chain and lock, and two signs-NO Trespassing and BEWARE of Dog. It was the perfect place to get away or to do something illegal.

Alan sipped at his coffee as the sun rose over the horizon high on this hill along the Potomac River that summer morn in 1995. *All those fools going to work downstream from here, down in Washington* he thought. Movement caught his eye. The spider he tried to kill earlier was back. It had spun a new web at the corner of the porch post and the roof timber. And it had just captured a victim, a wasp. Quickly, she danced over to her catch, and began to entomb him in a cocoon of silk. The wasp fought back, trying to sting her with his tail, but she carefully avoided his thrusts, and continued to encircle him with her silky threads. Soon all Alan could see was a cocoon that continued to struggle. Skillfully the spider crept close, and stung her prey. The wasp jerked and quickly was overcome by her poison. The spider now worked at securing the package to her web. She would slowly suck the juices and life from him in the days to come.

It was always so crisp after a storm, and they'd had a big one last night. The big sycamore tree that was near the house had blown over. The whole tree lay on its side with roots sticking at least six feet in the air. Alan thought that tree had probably seen many an Indian pass by as it was so old. Alan walked over to the horizontal remains of the tree. It was sad to see this behemoth of a tree laid low. There would be a lot of work to do to get this removed. Mike would be up soon. He would be surprised at the casualty. Alan circled the tree slowly. *What's that?* Something very rusty about three feet long laid half buried in the ground that the uprooting had exposed. He dug around one end with his hands and tried to lift it. *No way Jose, this thing must weight a ton.* It felt like it was solid lead. He'd need Mike's help with this.

"Would you look at that?"

Alan looked up. Mike was walking toward him and the downed tree.

"Must have been some storm, I slept right through it," he said.

Yes, Alan thought, *you slept right through it. After a fifth of Jack Daniel, you could sleep through the end of the world.* Alan knew what alcohol could do to a man. He'd seen it ruin his dad and his family. One day he would leave this old coot behind, but this wasn't the day. He still needed him. That time would come one day when the timing was right.

"How'd the trailers make out? Any damage to them from the storm?" Mike asked.

"Don't know, just got up and found the tree down and this old pipe," Alan replied.

"Looks like we've got a full day's work right here just cutting up the tree and getting rid of that rusty pipe. That's some tough wood, sycamore. We'll pile the wood over by that hole on the bank and burn it later. The pipe will go in the hole, but let's get breakfast first. And we better check the trailers before we eat. The Voice won't like it if any of his precious crop is ruined."

Alan nodded. No, the Voice would not like it if the grow houses were damaged. High-grade marijuana was bringing a premium price with the Feds watching the borders closely. And you didn't want to disappoint the Voice.

Chapter 7

Alan Grey sat on the porch sipping his cup of coffee. It had been two days since the big storm. The sunrays were peeking over the horizon and the warming rays would be hitting the old house that sat on the north end of Patterson Creek Ridge. No damage had been done to the old trailers that served as grow houses for the Voice. Alan liked to think about his life as the day dawned. *Oh, the places you'll go and the sights you'll see, Dr. Seuss had promised. Or was it more like that song like from the Grateful Dead? What a long strange trip it's been.* Both seem to fit his life. Growing up in the projects, drunken abusive father, poverty, juvenile jail, and sentenced to five years in prison for manslaughter. He would have received a lot longer sentence if the defense hadn't lost so much of the evidence.

He remembered his first day in prison. Big Tony had approached him and asked him if he needed protection. No, he said. He could take care of himself. He winced as he remembered the beating by the prison gang, the black prison gang. The guards just laughed. The next day as he nursed his wounds and bruises, Big Tony asked him again if he needed protection. This time he said yes. Big Tony said he would take care of it. Later in the day, Alan saw the leader of the group that had hurt him. His face looked like it had been smashed into a table repeatedly. Later at supper, Big Tony stopped at his table and said to him, "They won't bother you again. In here it's us versus them."

That was the day Alan learned to hate. As long as he hung with Big Tony and his group, no harm came to him. Alan became a model prisoner. He developed two faces, one for the guards and one for when he was alone with the other prisoners. He would serve whatever master he needed to survive. With gain time for good behavior, he got out at three years and six months. Big Tony and his group kept him safe. The day before the release Big Tony had talked to him. "You're gettin' out tomorrow, and they're gonna give you twenty bucks. How far you think you'll get on that? What you gonna do?"

Alan said he'd go see his mom, but he knew he couldn't stay there. His dad told him he never wanted to see him again. It still hurt what that s.o.b. had said.

Big Tony listened, and stated, "I know someone on the outside who can help you like I helped you in here if you're interested. Treat him fair, and he will help you. You don't want to cross him. Trust me. You don't want to cross him. I've seen what happened when you do. Interested?"

Alan said yes. Any friend of Big Tony's was a friend of his.

Big Tony responded, "He's not my friend, and he ain't gonna be yours. Think of him as a, as a business partner, only you're the junior partner. You don't want to make mistakes. You're expendable. Do well, and you can move up. Still interested?"

Alan said yes.

"Good," said Big Tony. "When you leave here, go down to the end of the block and look for the Grey Bar Restaurant. Sit at the bar. Ask the guy behind it for a Grey Bar Special. Tell him Big Tony sent you. You will get a breakfast and some further instructions. Follow them to the letter."

It had been as he said. He got a hardy breakfast. After he ate, the grizzled waiter placed a wallet and a cell phone on counter. He looked Alan hard in the eye. "There's $100 in that wallet. Don't get drunk with it. Don't use it for drugs. Keep the cell phone charged and on, always. Never, never ever use it for personal calls. Tomorrow you will get a call at 1300 hours, that's 1:00 p.m. to civilians. Answer it on the third ring. Got that?"

Alan said yes. He could remember it. He repeated it verbatim.

The grizzled waiter's eyebrows rose. He smiled. "I can see why Big Tony recommended you. You can do well with us, but remember this first and above all else. You don't ever wanta disappoint the Voice."

Chapter 8

Alan finished his breakfast, got up, and went to the bathroom. When he returned, he looked at his place at the bar. It had been wiped clean. There was nothing there, only a shiny counter.

"Hey," Alan said to the guy behind the counter, "What do I owe you?"

"Nothing," the man replied. "I'll put it on Big Tony's tab. Where you off to now, young man?"

"Home, wanna sees my mama," Alan answered.

"I hear that a lot, good luck, may you never spend a night up the road ever again," the man kidded.

"Which way to Interstate 70?"

"It's about one mile down that way," he pointed. "Stay on this street. You'll see the signs."

"Thanks," and with that he was out the door.

The walk felt good. It had been so long since he had walked that far in a straight line, no concrete block walls, or fences with razor wire to stop him. He went up to the interstate ramp and put out his thumb. He knew better than to hitchhike on the main road itself. A guy could get arrested, and he had no desire to go back ever. Many cars passed him by. None stopped. *Must know they're near a prison,* he thought. Finally a grey fairly-new Ford pickup stopped. A man of about fifty was driving. He rolled down the window and asked, "Where ya goin' son?"

"Hagerstown. You going that far?" he said hopeful for a ride.

"Well, what ya waitin' for? Get in," and get in Alan did.

He pulled onto the ramp and merged onto the highway going west.

Trying to be friendly, he asked the driver where he was going. He replied, "Well, it so happens I'm going up to West Virginia to look at some property my late, favorite Uncle Michael left me. Actually, I was named after him and was his only living heir. I hadn't seen him in years so it was a surprise when I got the call from the lawyer. Just the same, may he rest in peace. No more worries on this screwed up Earth for him. No more rat-race and the rats are winning."

To be polite, Alan said he was sorry to hear of the man's loss.

"And what about you son; what brings you out today?" he queried.

Alan flinched a little. *Here's where I get asked to get out of the truck.* "To be truthful with you, sir, I just got out of prison and I want to see my momma."

The man was silent for what seemed forever, though it was only a few moments. *He's probably thinking on how he can get rid of me,* Alan thought.

"Government, government, dang 'em all for good," he growled.

This was not the response Alan had anticipated. Somewhat surprised, Alan asked, "Why do you say that?"

With that, the floodgates open up. The man ranted, he raged, he whined on for ten minutes about what was wrong with the world. Government, all governments, the world would be so much better without them. They stole people's freedoms. They were the cause of all wrongs in this world. Taxes, out of control spending, giving money to people that didn't earn it, wars, mass murder, theft, wars, terrorism, etc., etc. On and on he went and kept going. Alan wondered if maybe he should ask to get out of the truck. Still he was heading toward Momma, and the man had made no threatening moves toward his young passenger.

Alan did what any good hitchhiker does. He nodded his head, and said he agreed with the driver. Alan thought, *if he wanted to be a Republican, I'll be one, too. If he wants to be a Democrat, I'll be one, too. If he wants to be an anarchist, I'll be one, too.*

Finally he was done his rant. Alan said he knew how he felt. He'd just gotten out from under the governments' oppressive thumb himself.

The man looked at Alan. "The name's Michael Levy, but most folks just call me Mike. If you're not doin' anything, don't think you've lined up a job yet, would you be interested in helping me fix up the place in West Virginia? I can't pay much, but you'd get a roof over your head and grub. The lawyer said the place needed work. It won't be the Hilton, but you can leave anytime you want. You'll have freedom young man, freedom."

Alan thought for a moment. The guys a little crazy, but he seems no threat to me. And no, he didn't have anything else to go. "Okay, I'm in, but first I want to see my momma. That road sign says my exit is in one mile. Can we stop there first?"

"No problem," he said. "No matter how old a son, he should try to take care of his momma." So off the interstate they went toward Momma's place.

Chapter 9

The ride to the church from Cindy's was less than a mile, and with no stoplights on Route 28, it went quick. Tom pulled his truck into the recently paved church parking lot. He got out and headed toward the church office door. Father Frank was there with his key, opening up. They went in. The Padre quickly moved to the new security panel and punched in the code. He said, "Don't know how long it'll take me to get use to this thing. What are things coming to? You would think people would have more respect for a church."

"Yes, you would," said Tom. "Have you gotten things back ship shape yet? It's been what, about a month?"

"Just a little over that. They did a lot of damage, but we had a lot of help in getting things back together. What the devil meant for evil, God meant for good. We had such a pouring out of support from the area churches, it was almost unbelievable. They provided money, labor, and lots of moral support after the church got trashed inside by the vandals. And this new security system with video surveillance was provided and installed by the people from the synagogue in Cumberland. Talk about a miracle. God really answers prayer," said the Padre with enthusiasm. "Take a look around."

Tom and Father Frank walked into the auditorium.

"Yes, you'd hardly know how much damage was done. This looks good as new, maybe better," Tom observed.

He walked over to the white board, nice and clean now.

"Yes, much better now," said Father Frank.

The last time Tom had seen it was just after the vandalism. In big bold letters was written NIGGER GO HOME on the board. Tom had asked the Padre about that. He said to him "You just got to forgive and move on." He knew this was where God wanted him, and he was not moving. He still had work to do here, and he was going to do it until God and the church higher ups saw fit to move him.

"Now," said Tom. "What was it you couldn't talk about over at the restaurant?"

The Padre began, "The Sunday the coin showed up in the offering, I forgot to turn off the surveillance cameras outside. The thing's so new, and I'm still on a learning curve with it. So I looked at the tapes of who came that day. It was just all locals, no visitors. The next Sunday I asked if anyone had dropped a special coin in the offering. No one said anything then, but the next day one of the women called and said her son had dropped it in as a tithe. You know how moms have a way of extracting information from little kids acting guilty."

Tom's eyes widened. The Padre looked at him knowingly, "that's right," he has nine more of them, actually eight now. He cut one up and used the pieces for fishing line sinkers. He's lost most of those pieces fishing."

"Nine, that's a small fortune!" Tom exclaimed.

"Yes, it is. Now you see why I didn't want to say more. I may have said too much at Cindy's already. I hope not," the Padre continued. "I told her to keep it quiet; the fewer people that know of this the better. She said her son Tim found the ten coins in a bag in the creek while fishing. She and Timmy want us to keep the coin. It was Tim's tithe offering to God."

"So now what? What do you do now?" Tom asked.

"I don't rightfully know what to do for the big picture yet, but I do know gold can bring out the worst in people. As it says in the Good Book, 'The love of money is the root of all kinds of evil.' I think we need to be careful."

Tom nodded, "I agree. We need to be careful."

After that, the conversation turned to things going on at the church, in the community, and finally the political scene coming out of Washington, D.C. Tom glanced at his watch. "Guess I'd better be going. Doug is probably thinking I got lost. I hope Joann told him I would be late."

The Padre mused, "Yes, you better had get a move on it. That's a fine son you have in Doug."

"That he is. I don't know where I'd be without him. He has been a life saver for our business," said Tom.

"You two work well together. Now get outta here. I'll be in touch. Take care," Father Frank chided.

"Will do, you take care, too." With that, Tom left the Padre and the church and headed for his truck. It'd been a full day so far. He wondered what more surprises the day held.

Chapter 10

The trip from Interstate 70 to Alan Grey's home in the projects was short. You could still hear the traffic, especially the big trucks rolling by on the super highway.

"This is it," said Alan. "If my old man's here, I won't be long. If Mom's here, could be a half hour. Is that okay with you?"

"Take your time. Ain't in no big hurry. Just wanta make it to see what kinda house and property my uncle left me before it gets late. We may have to turn on utilities and that will be hard in the dark, 'specially seein' we don't know where nothin' is," Mike pointed out. "You still comin' with me, right?"

"Yah, I'm coming. I won't be too long, 'specially if Dad's here," Alan said as he exited the truck. He walked to the row house, then up to the third floor apartment Alan had known as home. He hesitated in front of the door. *What kind of welcome would he get? Well,* he thought, *only one way to know.* He knocked on the door and heard stirring in the house. The door opened up. There was his momma.

"Momma, I...," that was all he got out of his mouth.

"ALAN!!!" Momma screamed out. Then she grabbed and hugged Alan so hard his ribs hurt. "Alan, Alan, Alan," she cried. "I wondered if I would ever see you again. BILLY!!! Come here! Your big brother is here."

A squeal came from the other room where the noise from a TV was coming. Then a young boy came running and grabbed Alan around the leg. "Alan!" he yelled. "Alan!"

Alan was overwhelmed and enjoyed every bit of it. "I said I'd come back, Momma, I said I'd come back." Then he looked around. "Where's Dad?"

"He went to the liquor store. He is as bad as ever, Alan. He won't like it if you're here," said Momma.

Alan looked around the apartment. It was even shabbier than he remembered. "I won't be here long, Momma. Just had to see you guys, you and Billy. Somehow I'll find a way to get you out of this place, somehow I will, Momma. You all been okay?"

"About the same, Alan. Still can't get your Dad to go to AA. He needs it so bad. It's killing him. He just won't stop drinking."

Momma went to the refrigerator to get some food for Alan. "I can't stay long, Momma, I got a man waiting for me out in the parking lot. I'm gonna do some work for him on a place he's got in West Virginia."

She talked him into staying for a sandwich, dill pickle, and soda. He ate and thanked her. Then he got up to leave. "Do you have to leave so soon?" she asked Alan.

"Don't want to, Momma, but Dad will be here soon, and Mike's waiting in his truck. I better go," said Alan. "Somehow, someway, I'll be back and get you out of this place. You deserve better than this. I promise; I'll be back."

Alan headed for the door and opened it. "I love you Momma," he said as he gave her a big good-bye hug.

"And I love you, too, Alan."

"Don't go Al, don't go," his little brother pleaded.

"I don't want to, but I got to little brother. I'll be back, I promise," Alan replied.

His mother let go of her son. "I know you will, I know you will," she said with tears in her eyes. Alan walked through the door that shut behind him. He was alone, and his heart ached. Somehow, he would find a way to get Momma and Billy out of this hellhole, somehow. He wiped a tear that ran down his cheek and walked down the steps to Mike's truck.

"That wasn't very long, everything okay?" Mike asked concerned.

"Yah," he said as he sniffed and cleared his throat. "Everything will be okay. Hey, don't we want to get there before dark? Let's get going."

"You okay?" Mike asked.

"Yah, I'm okay."

Mike pulled the truck out of the parking lot, and headed down the road to the Interstate.

Yah, Alan thought, *everything was going to be okay. Somehow, someway he would find a way, somehow.*

Chapter 11

The trip with Mike west on the interstate was uneventful. Lots of pretty farmland and woods Alan noted. *Wonder how far it is to Mike's late uncle's place?* Mike exited the four-lane highway in Cumberland and crossed the Potomac River into Wild, Wonderful West Virginia, or so the sign said. *State Route 28 was narrow and had more twists than a snake*, Alan thought, but when they turned on the Old Furnace Road, he found out what a crooked road really was. They passed the old iron furnace that sat across the road from the Old Furnace Church of the Brethren. They went up hills, down hills, up valleys, down valleys, turn left, turn right, and on and on for what seemed forever. Alan's stomach tightened up. *But it was only six miles.* It just seemed much, much longer. *Where were we now? What did that sign say? Welcome to the community of Patterson Creek, unincorporated.* They slowed to thirty-miles per hour as they went through the sleepy, little town. Mike turned right at an unmarked road and drove on past several barns and a herd of Black Angus cows that looked very healthy. And they smelled healthy, too. There was nothing like the smell of fresh manure to get your attention. Mike slowed as the road turned right and the creek came into view. Ahead was the low-water bridge. Alan had never seen one of these and said so to Mike. Mike nodded. "Not many of them around. They're only found on country roads that don't get a whole lot of use."

They stopped on the bridge and looked up and down the creek. It looked like a picture in an old-time magazine. After about a minute, Mike gave the truck some gas and off they went again. They traveled along the side of the creek, came to a sharp left turn, and then proceeded up the steep country road through a thick forest. The road had no centerline. At the top of the hill, the road had another sharp turn, this time to the right. At this point, the road straightened out and ran through a trough. Long ago, the road had been at the level of the surrounding thick woods, but years of erosion had put it at its present level. They traveled about another half mile and Mike turned left and stopped at a gate. He looked at Alan and said, "We're here. Well, almost. The house is just up this road."

He gave Alan a key and said, "Get the gate and make sure you lock it behind you."

Alan got out, walked to the gate, unlocked the lock, swung the gate open, and Mike drove through. Alan then shut and locked the gate. He walked to the truck, got in and said, "How much further? I don't see a house yet."

"Not much further. You can't see the house from the road. It's as I remember it. My uncle never married. He was a confirmed bachelor and kind of a hermit. He loved his privacy," Mike answered.

They drove on and soon came to a large field that sat on the plateau of the ridge they were on. "Hey, there it is," Alan pointed. They passed an ancient, huge sycamore tree and stopped in front of the old, in need of repair, farmhouse.

"Yup, that's about how I remember it. Not much, but it'll keep the rain off your head. Let's see if the utilities are on," Mike said.

They got out of the truck. Mike pulled a key from his pocket and opened the front door. The house smelled like one that had been closed up for some time. He flipped a light switch and a pole lamp came on. "That's a start, let's open some windows and air this place out."

They did and fresh air soon filled the house. The house had two small bedrooms, a living room, a tight bath that was probably once a pantry, and a kitchen that still was full of canned goods.

"Just like he left it," Mike said. "He went to work one day and dropped dead on the floor. Doctors said it was a heart attack. He went quickly, probably didn't even know what hit him. Hope I go as quick and peaceful. Now, wonder if we got any water."

Mike turned the faucet at the kitchen sink and water poured out. He smiled "Yup, just like he left it. I don't know if this is coming from a well or a spring. We'll find out tomorrow. Let's fix some of the grub. Uncle won't be needin' it. I'm tired and I'm hungry."

They heated some canned soup and fixed some coffee. Soon the sun was setting. They found a couple of old rocking chairs and moved them to the front porch. A breeze cooled them. A slight movement caught Alan's eye. A small spider was building a web on the porch. Mike walked to the truck and came back with a bottle of Jack Daniels. "Want a drink Alan?" he asked.

Alan declined. He thought of his dad. He'd seen what hard drinking would do to a man.

"No, not a drinker. Thanks anyway," he said with a fake smile on his face.

"If you want a snort, just say when. Got a big day tomorrow. Got to see what else is here, how much work we have to do to get this place ship shape," Mike said.

Mike and Alan sat there enjoying the solitude. Time passed as the frogs started their evening serenade. Mike downed half of the bottle. He rose slowly, a little unsteady, looked at Alan and said "it's been a long day. I'm hitting the sack. You take the back bedroom. I'll see you in the morning. Good night."

"Yah, good night," Alan replied. It had been quite a day, from the Grey Bar Hotel in the middle of town to the old house in the middle of nowhere. *Old geezer seems all right so far,* though Alan didn't like his drinking, *but what could he say? It was his place. And what of this cell phone in his pocket? Who was this person known as the Voice, and what did he want?* Tomorrow was another day, and now he was tired. Tonight he would get the most restful night of sleep he'd had in several years. The sounds of the night here in the county would lull him to dreamland. *Almost Heaven, West Virginia. Take me home, county roads.*

Chapter 12

Alan rose at sunrise, just as he had while in prison. Old habits are hard to break. He could have slept till noon if he wanted. There was no one here to make him get up and go with the daily rhythm of prison. He could hear Mike snoring in the other bedroom. He became aware of the emptiness in his stomach. *Wonder what Uncle Michael left for breakfast?* He slipped on his pants, shoes, and socks, and headed for the kitchen. There he found a bowl, silverware, a cup, corn flakes, and dried milk. He tasted the corn flakes, a little stale but edible. *What's this? Coffee!* He hadn't had any coffee since he went to prison. Quickly, he prepared his breakfast. *My, that coffee perking smelled like heaven.* He ate the bowl of cereal swiftly as was his habit in prison. The old Mister Coffee gave a final burp to let him know it was done. He rose and poured himself a cup. *Oh, yes, I have died and gone to heaven* he thought. The coffee tasted like nectar of the gods. It had been so long. He walked to the screen door. The sunrays streamed through. He could still hear Mike snoring. Opening the screen door, he stepped out on the porch and sat in the chair. He noticed a spider web clinging to the porch center post. The sunshine made the dew-damp gossamer treads shine brightly. It was a chamber of commerce morning. He would see many of them from this porch. After sitting for a few minutes, just enjoying his newfound freedom, he got up. *I wonder what this place looks like?* he thought. He walked around the old house and took in the big picture of his surroundings. It was chilly that spring morning. He saw an old house, two doublewide, big, ancient trailers, a large shed in the same condition as the house, and a little building out in the field, probably a well house. And two old windmills going round and round. That was the sound he could not identify last night. Up here on this ridge, there must always be a breeze. He would find he was right about that a majority of the time.

He peeked into the trailer, empty, totally empty, no walls, no furniture, no bath, nothing in it either, just four walls. The unlocked shed had lots of plastic pipe of various sizes, large plastic bags, assorted tools, a large number of what he thought were fluorescent lights, and a huge number of industrial sized batteries all wired together. With his curiosity satisfied, he walked out and shut the door behind him. Off in the distance he heard a low rumble that was getting louder. He walked past the windmills to the tree line. There he found a cliff going nearly straight down one hundred feet to the railroad tracks he could see through the trees. He watched a train rumble by with its open cars full of coal and limestone gravel. It disappeared out of view, and he heard it whistle at a distant crossing somewhere. After that, he walked back to the house and heard Mike still snoring in bed. He got the last of the coffee. *How had he lived without it in prison? What should he do now?* He walked back out the door and surveyed the large field there on the plateau on the ridge. There was only one tree in the field, the ancient sycamore with its peeling bark in the field. He walked out the lane to it. This thing must be as old as Methuselah. He marveled at its size. *Now what to do?* He decided to walk to the main road. He climbed the gate and looked down the secondary road both ways. It didn't look like it got much traffic ever. It was far different than what he had known in the city. He pulled the cell phone out of his pocket. Yes, he had service. He didn't see any towers on the distant hills. *Got to be one close somewhere.* He looked at the time feature on the phone, ten o'clock. He wondered what the Voice would have to say when he called. His stomach churned a little.

Hey, what's this? There was a newspaper stuck in the green plastic box. *Cumberland Times News* was printed on the side. Mike must have ordered it. He grabbed the newspaper and looked at the front page, same old stuff, war, killing and corruption. Good news just doesn't sell papers. He climbed up over the gate and headed for the farmhouse. He could see Mike sitting on the front porch. As he got close to the house, he cried out "It's about time you got up. Did you sleep tight? You were sure snoring."

Mike smiled. "Yah, I slept like a baby. Sorry about the snoring. I got my nose broke as a kid, and have snored ever since. Did you find some breakfast? I think my uncle left this place stocked up with supplies. He didn't leave this place often."

"Yah, I found some corn flakes, dried milk, and fixed some coffee," said Alan.

"Coffee! I'm so glad you found the coffee,' exclaimed the older man. "Did you get a look around the old place?"

"Yah, lot more here than what meets the eye," he responded. "Let me get you some coffee. I figured out how the coffee maker works. I got some for myself while you were still sleeping."

"Thanks," Mike said. "You do that, and then we need to talk."

Alan had been expecting that. Mike would spell out his plans for the old place, and what he needed Alan to do. He prepared the coffee for Mike. It was ready in a jiffy. He brought the big, steaming cup of java to Mike. Mike took it and sipped. "Ah, that's good, really good."

"Now what was it you needed to talk with me about?" Alan asked satisfied he knew what was coming.

Mike sipped the coffee, than looked sternly at Alan. "At 1300, that's 1:00 p.m.. for civilians, you will get a call on that cell phone in your pocket."

Alan's eyes widened, and his jaw dropped. This was not what he expected from Mike.

Mike continued, "You will get instructions and an offer. You can walk away if you want at this point, but I think it would be very profitable and in your best interest if you take it. The Voice has been good to me. He's fair, and working for him has been very profitable for me. But this you must remember, above all else you must remember, don't ever, ever disappoint the Voice."

Mike looked at the stunned young man. Even Alan's experience at hiding his feelings he learned in prison had not prepared him for this. "You didn't really think my picking you up there on the interstate ramp was sheer chance, did you?"

Mike let him think on that for a few seconds. "Everything has a reason. Everything is connected. Don't forget this."

Alan recovered somewhat and stammered, "Who is this Voice?"

Mike shrugged his shoulders. "Don't really know, but never disappoint him. It's not healthy."

Alan sat back in the chair. *Who was this Voice, and what had he gotten himself into?*

"Was there anymore coffee left in the pot?" Mike questioned.

"Yah, about a half cup," Alan answered.

"Good, I need a warm up." With that Mike got up and headed for the kitchen leaving Alan to his thoughts. *Just what had he got himself into? And where would this lead?* Time would tell, and he had a decision to make.

Chapter 13

Mike came back several minutes later with his coffee cup full. "Good coffee, I made another pot," he said matter of fact like.

"Yah, good coffee, I found a can that had never been open this morning," Alan responded.

Mike sat back down in the chair. He looked at Alan. "Guess you're wondering about who the Voice is, and what he wants of you?"

Alan nodded.

"To be completely truthful with you, I don't know who he is, nor am I sure I want to know. Whoever he is, he has power and connections. When you left prison did they talk to you about parole?" Mike asked.

"No," Alan answered.

"Didn't you think that a little strange, you being a convicted felon?"

"Yes, I did," Alan said.

Mike began, "The Voice took care of it for you. Like I said, he has power and connections. I don't know how far his tentacles reach, but I wouldn't want to try to out run them. I know you have been looking the place over. You notice how isolated we are here. You've seen the empty double wide trailers, and the stuff in the shed, the plastic pipe, and the batteries. My uncle ran a marijuana grow house up here for the Voice for some years till he started getting sick. It was very profitable for him, but what he did with his money, I don't know. He didn't put it in this house, and, it was not in his will. I don't know if he buried it here, burned it, or gave it away. After he got ill and couldn't run the grow house, the Voice pretty much put him out to pasture right here. The Voice is fair if you do him right. What he wants from you and me is to set up the grow house operation in the old trailers out there. He wants two people so when one needs to leave, this place is always manned. He will provide the money we need while here for this operation. At the end when the crop is harvested and out of here, we get our cut of the profits. I've never known anyone to not have been treated fairly by the Voice. That's how he keeps his troops happy and loyal. You might see him as a benevolent dictator. He prefers the carrot, not the stick, but he carries a big stick. You know, a little like old Teddy Roosevelt, 'Walk softly and carry a big stick.'"

Alan looked at Mike and mulled all this over in his mind.

Mike continued, "I'm gonna need to go into town and get some supplies. That will give you some time to think. When he calls at 1300 answer promptly, be polite, and tell him if you're in on this operation. There will be no opting out until it's done. You think on it."

Shortly afterward, Alan would watch the truck with Mike in it disappear down the two tire worn country lane to the state road. *What would he do? Did he want to be in on this? How much money would he get?* Enough for him, maybe enough to help Momma. He weighed the pros and cons. This Voice had to have connections to have gotten him off without having to do parole. And he had to know how people thought when he so slyly had Mike pick him up at the interstate ramp. He was good, but also dangerous. Power hadn't gone to his head, and from what Mike said, he knew how to use it. Alan didn't think he wanted to find out first hand.

When the call came at 1300 hours, Alan had made his decision. Yes, he was in till the crop was harvested. The Voice was pleased. He told him he would profit handsomely if all went well. Think of it like profit sharing the Voice had said.

Treat him fairly, and he would treat you fairly. At the end of the conversation, the Voice gave the veiled threat, "Don't disappoint me, I don't handle disappointment well."

Alan was sure he didn't. It had been somewhat unnerving talking to the computer enhanced and altered voice that came to his ear. This was a person of power, means, and ways.

This was not a person you wanted to disappoint.

It was late in the afternoon when Mike pulled up the farm lane. The back of the truck was full of plant potting mix, and the cab was full of groceries. Alan went out to the truck and said to the returning Mike, "I'm in."

Mike smiled and answered, "Yah, I know. You made a smart move. I was afraid I would have to kill you."

Alan smiled sheepishly. *Was he kidding or not?*

"Give me some help with this stuff. I got some cold stuff in that one bag, and it's getting warm. Get it in the fridge. We'll unload the stuff in the back of the truck later. Let's get some supper. Hope you like Chinese," Mike said.

Alan quipped, "Chinese restaurants, they're everywhere."

"Yup, even in Jerusalem," Mike added. "We'll get started on the operation tomorrow. When you go down to get the paper tomorrow morning, look for a brown paper bag hidden in the weeds by the road. It will have inside a plastic container filled with the best genetically modified polyploidy pot seed this side of Vietnam."

The next morning, just as Mike had said, the paper bag with the plastic container was there and full of seeds. This was one efficient operation. Alan knew he had made the right decision, but a little doubt remained. He would do his share and then some. He hoped there would be enough to help his momma. That was his plan. That was his motivation. And he knew he did not want to disappoint the Voice.

Chapter 14

Tom pulled the old truck out of the Catholic Church parking lot space and stopped at Route 28. He looked south down the road and noticed the church marquee, "Choose life," it said. Father Frank believed in expressing his faith. Where had the Supreme Court ever found a right to abortion in the Constitution? Forty million dead and still climbing. America was killing its future. How different the nation would look if those missing people were here? God must be weeping. Tom reasoned the Supreme Court found it at the same place they found separation of church and state, even though none of these words are in the Constitution. Why old Thomas Jefferson who wrote the Constitution approved, at government expense, the use of Hymnals and Bibles as schoolbooks. Government buildings were used on Sunday for church services. *I guess that's what you get with a 'living Constitution,'* Tom thought. *That's like trying to build on quick sand. Quick sand is 'living'. Give me the unchanging solid rock. That's the right foundation for a country, or a life.* He was glad he had friends like the Padre. There were days in his life when he felt he was being pulled through a knothole. He paused for an additional minute. He thought of what Father Frank had put up after the vandalism at the church. *All things work together for them that love the Lord.* The Church and community had really come together after the destruction. Things had worked out. It was harder to see with other events, like his son and wife's deaths. He had learned more compassion for hurting people, but at a terrible cost. Maybe he wouldn't understand till he made it to heaven. Some things are like that. He used to think taking one's life was an unforgivable sin, but now he realized there was only one--- rejecting Jesus as Savior and Lord. He understood how death could be an illogical choice in the mind of a person with mental illness. It was an escape from the confused madness they must live with. He took a deep breath and eased his way on to the highway.

As the truck crossed the small bridge over Turners Run, he wondered what else would happen today. He thought of all the people who had been maimed or killed on bloody Route 28 as he cruised toward Short Gap. *When would the state ever improve this road?* A couple hundred feet of new guardrail would not solve its many problems. So many lives had been cut short on this heavily used highway. He rounded the turn in Short Gap, and passed the old Methodist Church, now boarded up. The present owner was using it for storage. It sure could use a coat of paint. The Methodists moved to their new church off Rt. 956 years ago. He slowed for a car turning left onto Route 956, then by the road leading up to Frankfort High School. Senior Class Play this Friday at 7:00, "My Fair Lady" the sign read. After the long straight stretch, Tom rounded a moderate turn. He remembered a wreck at that spot years ago. Two guys from school were feeling invincible, bullet proof, and immortal from too much testosterone, alcohol, and speed. They missed the turn and ended up putting the souped up Pontiac on its side among the numerous trees. How they got out alive with barely any scratches would never be known. No seat belts and a tree through the windshield of the overturned car. People said it was a miracle no one was killed. This accident was driver error. He couldn't lay the fault of a bad road on this one. Another mile and he would be home. He turned left at the Hunt Club Plaza. His family had owned the land on both sides of this road. Some they had to sell off when things were tough just to get by, but somehow they had always made it through. Tough times don't last, but tough people do. The Lord will provide what you need. The Lord will provide. On this promise he could depend. He pulled the truck up onto his property, turned the engine off, and sat in the quiet of his truck. His mind was on a roll. There was much more thinking to do.

Chapter 15

Yes, those were some tough time. The big plants were shutting down in the area, Celanese, PPG, and his job place, Kelly Springfield Tires. It seemed like you couldn't buy a job around the Tri-state area. He was glad they had the old farm. Tom sold off some land for the commercial center where the credit union located. They had been good to him, and the business he had started. He sold some more land off to the Knotts Brothers, and they built homes and some buildings for their business. Tom sometimes had to pinch himself to believe how his fortunes had turned, though not without many challenges from many sources.

The state, back in the days when Motel T's traveled the road in front of the house, had built a trough to catch water from the big spring that poured out of the mountain, Knobley Mountain that rose up sharply about 500 feet behind the old barn behind the farmhouse that sat next to the highway. People stopped to water their overheated cars in the old days, and then got water for themselves, too. Tom's dad had stuck a can up next to the trough which was on his property with a sign that said "money for water." He was amazed that people actually gave. It wasn't much, but it helped especially in the hard days of the depression. The state said he couldn't charge for the water, so he changed the sign to "donations for water." It took a year, but they said he couldn't do that either. So Tom's dad just left the can up and took down the sign. People still gave.

After Tom lost his job at Kelly, he looked into bottling the water for sale. No one encouraged him except for his good wife, Sarah. She was his rock, always believing in him. No one wanted the water in their store. They had plenty they said. Who was he to think he could compete with the big boys? Now the big boys wanted to buy him out. What a change of fortune. How many government agencies with all their regulations had tried to stop him? No wonder the companies were moving to China. He was so glad he had a lawyer friend from good old Fort Ashby High School days that helped him fight them, and as a favor to a friend, was willing to wait for his money that may never come. Tom had paid him back with interest and made sure his office always got bottled water for free. The lawyer always smiled and asked for a bill. Tom's employee was always told to tell him they would mail it. They never did or would. Tom had been able to get some bottling equipment from the old Queen City Brewing Company when it shut down, and that had surely helped.

He laughed to himself how he got him first account, Wayne's Grocery in Fort Ashby. He talked to Wayne, but he had said he had no need for another bottled water, even if it was a local one called Knobley Mountain Spring Water. Tom was desperate. He had used all money he had to get this started, and now no one wanted his product. That day he sat at the house and put an old cassette by Sammy Hall in the tape player. Tom could still hear Sammy singing in his mind, "If nobody loves you, create the demand." Those words in the song were the key he needed that day. Tom contacted the Mineral County Fair directors. He would give them all the bottled water they needed Monday night for free if they would buy bottled water from him exclusive at his costs for the rest of the week. They agreed, and thus demand began. Tom had printed on the bottle's labels, "Knobley Mountain Spring Water, available at Wayne's Grocery and other quality stores in the Tri-state area." Under that was the company's address and phone number. Tom remembered the call from Wayne the next day because he had taken it. "You dog, you dirty dog," Wayne had laughed. "I got bunches of people over here wanting to know where that

'Knobley Mountain Spring Water' is in my store, and I ain't got it. Bring me two pallets right now, and I will put it right at the door for all to see. And I need it now!"

Tom said he would bring it over ASAP. He had anticipated the calls, and had the truck loaded fully. Wayne got his load within the hour. The rest of the day he was busy answering calls, taking orders, and doing deliveries. It had mushroomed from there. Now he, his two sons, new wife Joann, and four other employees were on the pay roll of Knobley Mountain Spring Water. He had been blessed. When given a lemon, make lemonade. Tom got out of the truck, and walked into the office. "Hey, Dad," his son Doug said, "Glad you got here. We got a big order we need delivered today. Everyone else is busy. We need you to get it out today."

"That's great news. Why needs the rush order?" Tom asked.

"Your favorite place, Dad."

"No, don't tell me I just volunteered for White Tails?" Tom groaned.

"Right as usual, Popster," Doug replied.

White Tails. Good account, they always paid by check on delivery. And a good check at that. But White Tails? Why didn't they give the delivery to the naive new driver as they always did for fun? Tom smelled a conspiracy and said so.

"No, Dad, they called about an hour ago. You know they always wait till the last minute," replied Doug.

Tom knew this was true. White Tails. It was his lucky day. White Tail Nudist Resort needed water for an event, and he was going to get his eyes full. *Why me?* Tom thought. Seeing lots of naked people, most of them baby boomers full of wrinkles, sags, and bags, was not his idea of a fun time. They always sent the new, unknowing drivers for this chore. One had even wanted to quit. They talked him out of it only by promising him he would never have to go there again.

"Oh, alright, I'll be the sacrificial lamb. Which truck?" Tom conceded.

"Here are the keys, Dad. Have a nice day," Doug said with a chuckle in his voice.

Tom walked out the door and to the truck. It was loaded and the invoice for the water was on the seat. He started the truck, and pulled it down the drive to Route 28. He waited for some traffic and eased the big truck onto the highway south bound. *White Tails. It was turning into a very interesting day.*

Chapter 16

Tom drove the truckload of bottled water through the little town of Short Gap on WV 28. As he neared the cut off to Frankfort High School, his growling stomach reminded him he hadn't had lunch. *What time is it,* he thought? He glanced at his watch, 1330. One thirty, no wonder he was hungry. *Guess I'll stop at Cindy's again. She can get me a quick meal and then back on the road.* As he passed Route 956, he glanced right up the road. There was the gap in Knobley Mountain that the town was named for, the short gap to the Potomac River valley in Maryland. Tom wondered how many Indians had traveled this way long before the white settlers came. And how many of the latter had gone through there on their way west. Back in the late 1700s this whole region must have been busy with travelers going west. *Oh, if the rocks could talk, what stories could they tell?* By now Tom was passing Father Frank's church. *A good buddy that Padre.* On he drove into Fort Ashby, passed through the traffic light on a green, and he pulled into the lot at Cindy's. *Man*, he though, *this parking lot is full. What's going on in sleepy little Fort Ashby*? Luck was with him. Two cars end to end were leaving the parallel parking spots, and Tom pulled the big truck in and took up both spots.

He got out of the truck and walked to the door. He said hello to the two old gray-haired ladies leaving the restaurant, and they returned his greeting. He was very surprised when he got through the door. The place was packed. Cindy the owner came up to greet and seat him. "Hey, Tom, back again so soon?" she asked.

He smiled, "got hungry again. Why, what's going on? Don't think I've ever seen this place so full. What's going on?"

"Frontier days at the old fort. It's open. They got re-enactors; colonials, redcoats, and Indians, and such. Didn't you know? Weren't you head of the Sons of the American Revolution at one time?" she replied.

"Wow! No, I didn't know. I've been so busy with the water business. I stepped down a while back. Hey, can you get me something tasty quick? I'm on a special delivery run," he asked.

She took him to the overflow room and seated him. "I can get you a hot beef sandwich with mashed potatoes and covered with gravy in two shakes of a lamb's tail. That be fast enough?"

"Sounds super, Cindy. You're the best. If I wasn't married, I'd grab you up in a heartbeat," Tom kidded.

"Tom, someday I'm gonna swat you," she said with a smile. "You haven't been in this section for several years. You remember last time that little old man was asking if I knew of anyone who knew about local history in colonial times. Do you remember that?"

Tom's face went blank as he tried to remember. "Why yes, I had completely forgotten about that."

Cindy asked, "Were you able to help him? What did he want to know?"

Tom searched the remote areas of his brain. "He said he lived down near Patterson Creek. Let's see. He said his name was Mike, mmm, Mike something. I remember, Michael Levy and he wanted to know about," Tom paused, "Braddock's Gold. I can't believe it. That's twice today that topic has come."

"Must be an omen," Cindy mused.

"Yah, weird ain't it? Hey, where's my lunch? I could eat a horse," said Tom.

"No need for that. I have it here in a minute," she said, and it was.

Tom ate quickly. Ten minutes later he was back in the truck heading for White Tails.

Soon he was up and over Middle Ridge and heading down the other side toward Springfield. He went under the old railroad bridge that the B & O Railroad had sold to the state of WV. The state was now keeping it up for the farmers in the South Branch of the Potomac River who needed it for supplies. The tourist train, the Potomac Eagle, also used it to take people up through the Trough. It was like a wilderness. Here the river flowed between two parallel mountains. Tom and his wife had gone on it one day and saw bald eagles there. *What a great day we had,* he thought. He took a left onto the road to Green Spring. It went through a beautiful valley. Almost Heaven, West Virginia.

Tom thought of the little old man named Michael he had talked to. It was strange how the same subject had come up out of the blue, Braddock's Gold. Tom did some of his best thinking behind a steering wheel, but today he couldn't make a connection. Oh well, some things in life are just meant to be lived, not explained.

He slowed for the one lane toll bridge across the Potomac River. There was no one on the bridge so he proceeded. *I don't want to know what the weight limit for this thing is*, he thought. He paid the toll at the little toll booth, and drove on into Oldtown, Maryland. There was so much history in this area—the Shawnee Indians had a village here long ago. Here Cresap had his blockhouse trading post where young George Washington would see his first Indians. Braddock's Redcoats would travel through here before being defeated by the French and Indians in the Battle of the Monongahela near present day Pittsburgh, Pennsylvania. And through here again they would go in retreat without the now dead General Braddock. Here also the skirmishes and battles of the Civil War that had taken place. *Oh if the rocks could just talk, what stories they would tell,* Tom thought.

He got on Maryland Route 51 and headed east. Soon he was crossing back into West Virginia at Paw Paw on WV Route 9. He rode two miles to the sign that read Seymour Bottom Road.

How ironic, he thought, *a nudist resort on Seymour Bottom*. Old Man Seymour had owned and farmed the flat land here where the Potomac River made long and wide horseshoe turns. Tom had heard of the nudists taking half-day trips on this isolated section of the river. He turned left and was soon at the gate of White Tails. The guard came out of his hut. "They called me and said you would be coming. You got a load of water for the music concert this weekend," he said.

Tom responded, "Yes, I do. Hey, you were here last time I was here, only you greeted me in the buff."

"Yah, that was me. I only did it for 3 days. The bugs like to eat me up out here, and I got sunburn in places I don't want to talk about," he grinned. "I'm not gonna try that again."

"Understood," Tom said. "This is the kind of place where when they say 'good to SEE you' they really mean it."

The guard chuckled at that.

Tom asked, "Do you ever get any celebrities here? Can you tell me?"

The guard looked over his shoulder to make sure they were alone. "Yes, we do."

Tom asked, "Anyone you can tell me?"

The guard began "Well, I'll not name names, but last weekend we had a female member of the President's cabinet here. Boy, oh boy, did she have some thunder thighs. I wish I had never seen that. But you do kind of get used to it working here."

"Why do you work here?" asked Tom.

"I need a job and jobs are scarce now. The pay's not bad and they have good insurance that covers me and my family," the guard replied. "Better get moving. There's two cars pulling up behind you. Have a nice day."

"Be seeing you," Tom kidded as he drove off.

The guard grinned. Tom drove off to the warehouse where he would drop off the water. He only got his eyes half full on the way. No Greek Gods out today, just the usual big bellies and saggy well, whatevers. He backed up to the unloading bay. The manager was coming out and he walked up to the truck. "Good to see you made it here okay, but where's the rest of the water? That's only half the load."

All Tom could say was, "What?"

The manager continues, "I called and doubled the order about two o'clock. Didn't you get the message?"

"No, I was already on the road," Tom said. "It wouldn't have mattered anyway. All my trucks were busy, and this is the biggest delivery truck I've got. I tell you what. If you can get this off my truck in 15 minutes, I can get another load of water and be back by six o'clock. How's that sound?"

"Sounds good to me. I have someone here at six. I'll be gone so here's your check for the full amount. I trust you. You're an honest man. That's why I deal with you. And your product is Number One," the manager said.

They unloaded the truck with the fork lift quickly and Tom was back on the road. This time he stayed on Maryland Route 51 all the way to Cumberland. There he got on WV Route 28 and headed to his bottled water warehouse. This route seemed a little faster. He would remember that. His truck was quickly loaded and he was off again. He took the same way there, Route 28 to Cumberland then to Paw Paw via Maryland Route 51. He got there at five minutes to six. The warehouse man was waiting. "I knew you could do it," he said.

Tom's truck was swiftly unloaded and he was off toward home. He pulled into the warehouse behind his house at seven thirty. He was tired and hungry. It had been a full, but interesting day. *I wonder what tomorrow will bring*? Tom thought. *Lord, You are my strength. How could I ever do it without you*?

Chapter 17

George Washington's Personal Writings

These are some of the events that took place recently during my adventure in 1748 while surveying for James Genn. The gentleman sponsoring this project was Lord Fairfax. He was to oversee the surveying of lands in the valley of the South Branch of the Potomac he owned that he wished to sell for a profit.

As I am only 16, I felt fortunate to have been asked to participate, though I received no pay, only sustenance during the time beyond the Blue Ridge Mountains. I first learned the basics of surveying at the suggestion of my older brother, Laurence, who had become a substitute father to me after the untimely death of our father, Augustine, five years ago. He had suggested a career in the British Navy, but my mother had forbidden this. I was surprised when she consented to my going. Perhaps she realized I am nearly a grown man and knows she must soon let go the apron strings she holds me with. I wish to do so much, but she will have her say until I am twenty-one.

Still I believe I can see her point. We have seen many mothers weep when their young men went marching off never to return. I believe she felt I would be safe among the surveying party.

We left Tidewater, Virginia March 11, 1748. Soon we were beyond the orderly plantations and came to an area on the Occoquan Creek that was only a step above wilderness. Mr. Genn met us on the road to Frederick Town that some are now referring to as Winchester. We traveled over the Blue Ridge Mountains and stayed at the house of Captain John Ashby. He operated a ferry on the Shenandoah River. There was much rich land suitable for farming that Lord Fairfax owned and wanted surveyed. Our main camp was in Winchester. As there are many high mountains between there and the South Branch, a roundabout route was chosen to circumvent the high mountains. We proceeded north to the Potomac near the mouth of the Shenandoah, but found the river to be in flood stage so we were unable to cross. The decision was made to proceed on the south side of the river to Warm Springs also known as Bath. These springs were claimed to have healing powers, but we did not bathe in the pools.

Near Warm Springs we were able to cross the Potomac to the Maryland side. It rained constantly as we proceeded over what I would only describe as the worst road ever trod by man or beast. That day March 21, we were able to make into Thomas Cresap's place. Cresap was a renowned frontiersman respected by Whites and Red men both. His well-stocked trading post at Shawnee Oldtown was half house and half fort. The next day we wished to cross the river back into Virginia, but the water was too high and dangerous. That day, thirty Indians appeared at the trading post. Cresap inquired and found out they were a war party, but had been chagrined as their expedition had not been profitable. All they had to show for their efforts was one scalp. Our party gave the Indians a friendly offering of liquor which they gladly accepted. This raised their spirits. They built fires and prepared a dance. The dance was very interesting with all the shouting and jumping around. I have described it often for friends back home. One Indian was named Black Wolf. He had a wine stain birthmark on his face and was ever so slightly pigeon-toed. Cresap had advised me to steer clear of him, as he had a very bad disposition. I noted that his fellow warriors carefully and skillfully avoided crossing him.

By March 25, the river had dropped sufficiently for the horses to swim across. The men used canoes provided by Cresap. We crossed at a point opposite Patterson Creek without incident. By nightfall, we arrived at the farm of Abram Johnston where we were made welcome and spent the night.

Early the next morning something very interesting happened. Out of the woods came a man dressed more Indian than White. I had been talking with Mr. Johnston when this took place. Mr. Johnston saw him coming and seemed to have no concern. Out of curiosity, I asked who that was. "Lightfoot," he responded. "His family was settlers west of here. The Indians took him as a child and raised him. You won't find a soul that knows more about these woods in any direction or about fightin'. I'm glad we're on friendly terms. I wouldn't want to cross him, but he's a pretty good guy once you get to know him."

As he got closer, I could see he had three fresh scalps hanging from his side. He went with Mr. Johnston into the house where the others were. There he was introduced to the members of our survey team. They talked about their orders, business, the weather, and what not. Genn commented of just coming from Cresap's place and seeing a war party there. This interested Lightfoot. He asked if there were about thirty Indians. We said yes. He pointed to the scalps and said, "There used to be thirty-three. They knew better than to come in this area while I am here."

This brought a laugh from the men in the room. At this point, Genn asked Lightfoot if he was interested in traveling with us to the upper South Branch. Surprisingly, he agreed. He was to be provided food, power, shot, and rum for his pay. Just what he was to do was never discussed, but he acted as a scout and protector. He earned his pay several times over. I learned much from him. I studied him intensely. Never had I met someone like him.

   We left the next day and traveled further up the creek to the home of Solomon Hedges. The following day we left the creek and traveled east to the South Branch Valley. We passed over several hills and then down a fair-sized stream with good fall. It would make a good place for a future mill. At the creek's mouth into the South Branch we were accosted by a peculiar and most vile man on the island in the stream. He bade us to stay away with the most wretched of language. Soon we reached Mr. Pearsalls. He asked how our journey was from Patterson Creek. We replied it most agreeable except for the odd man we had met a short while ago. Mr. Pearsall laughed and referred to the disagreeable man as Old Piss Pott. He was a cantankerous hermit who lived on the island and wanted no contact with other people. With that exception, we had a grand time at the Pearsalls. By the end of the month, we were at our desired destination and began our surveying. This took two weeks. We were deep in the mountainous wilderness. The valleys and streams all ran parallel between the mountains. Lightfoot kept a ready eye for danger. Twice he disappeared into the woods for a day. Each time when he returned, he had a fresh scalp at his side. Everyone saw these. Nothing needed to be said of the dangers around us. We also saw a mother bear with two cubs, a mountain lion, deer, turkeys, and several buffalo. On the way back from our journey to Winchester, we stopped at the home of John Edwards near the Cacapehon, also spelled Cacapon River. It was a most beautiful area.

   While there on the grand adventure, we got wet and cold. The nights were long and smoky from camp fires. But I saw much land good for settling. I learned to run a line in the wilderness. I camped out, but must learn more on this as it was not to my satisfaction. Food was cooked over an open fire. We slept in the open, met Indians, and saw some of the dangers of the wilderness. I saw fine western land, the frontier. We even were followed for two days by German settlers who spoke less

English than the Indians. And I met Lightfoot, a man who would play an important part in my life, but for now I did not know that. All I knew was I was glad to be home from my adventure. I thought it best to leave out the part about Lightfoot so as not to worry my mother. You know how a mother can be, and I did not need to give her any more issues.

Chapter 18

Spring 1754

Lightfoot stood over the body of the Indian he had just killed, a Shawnee. Blood oozed from the dead man's wounds. A second dead Shawnee also lay near, just over the ridge. They had been following two British foot soldiers and a Colonial youth who had been unaware of their Indian shadows. He had no love for Redcoats, but he did not hate them either. The youth he knew as one who roamed the woods and trapped animals for fur. They had met in the woods sometime ago, had camped and hunted together and become friends, and more. Lightfoot had made him a blood brother. For this reason he killed the pursuing Shawnee. He would not take their scalps. There was nothing to prove, nor any of his people left to show his skills to. He did not care if their spirits followed him. There were too many memories and spirits following him already. Two more would only add to the long line. He would take their food, guns, powder, ammo, and knives. These had value to him. The guns had probably been traded by the dead men for furs the French wanted.

For now, he would follow the three discretely as only an Indian could. He would protect them from any more attacks on the trail from Winchester to Fort Ohio and Fort Cumberland. And they would never know he was there until he wanted his presence to be known. He would do it for the young man. He would let the youth catch fleeting glimpses of him over the next day or so, then disappear like a bird in the forest. The youth was good, but he still had much to learn if he wanted to be a *coureur de bois*, a runner of the woods, as the French would say. He must learn to live, speak, and think like an Indian if he was to survive. He must learn of pain, both to the body and soul, and to be soft as fur and hard as a stone. But now Lightfoot would feast on the dead men's food and then rest. There would be no problem picking up the three men's trail, especially the British. Today had gone well for Lightfoot, the White Indian.

Lightfoot reflected on his life. His parents had left eastern Virginia, crossed the mountains, and settled in the wilderness on the banks of the Youghiogheny River. He was born in a cabin there. He remembered his white name, John Lightfoot. Most of all he remembered his mother, the color of her hair, her smile, and of how hard she worked at the cabin. He remembered his new little brother, born just before he John was taken by the last of the Monongahela Indians. Was he still alive? If so, where was he? His Mother was always talking about the Bible, love thy neighbor, no stealing, tell the truth, and David, the warrior king. He would have made a good Indian this David. She talked also about this Jesus man. His six-year-old mind did not understand much about this Jesus, but Momma surely loved Him. She sang about Him while she worked. Someday he would learn more of this man who influenced his mother. He must be the one the Indians called the Master of Life or the Great Being. He remembered how the Indians grabbed him as he played in a stream and taken him to their village over several mountains and a river. Their village, their tribe, only had about forty people left. War raids by the Iroquois and famine from the past droughts had decimated their numbers. Any new blood was welcomed. They gave him the name Monacaloga. He spent seven years there learning to be an Indian. He had nearly forgotten his English till a British trader visited the tribe and provided much needed European goods.

He was now thirteen. Again his life would change. Tuscarora warriors aligned with the Iroquois massacred what was left of the Monongahela tribe. They had been killing anyone who was living on what they considered their lands, settlers included. He was only spared from the circling warriors because they were curious of his white skin and wavy auburn hair and his bravery. An important man of the Tuscarora stepped in and claimed him to replace a son he had lost to disease. He gave him the name White Thunder. Someday he would kill the brave he watched kill his Monongahela family, a family he had loved. One day he did. After five more years living and learning the ways of the Tuscarora and Iroquois, the day had come. A fur trader arrived with large amounts of rum and other goods. He got many animal skins in exchange. That night while the warriors were drunk, he found a tomahawk and sank it deep into the head of the one who killed his Indian family. And then he slipped away into the night and disappeared in the near-endless forest. If there had been pursuit, it hadn't gone far. He knew how to cover his tracks Indian style.

Now he lived between the parallel hills and valleys of Virginia among the few settlers who were there. Why were the two Shawnee men he killed wearing war paint? He needed to know. But for now he would creep near to the White men and watch over them tonight. Tomorrow would be when he showed himself and he would do it in a convincing way. He smiled to himself. He knew where and how, and he would make it very interesting, yes, very interesting.

Chapter 19

As Lightfoot continues to shadow the three young men, he contemplated his mission. He left his home near Patterson Creek when asked to discretely watch over the young man, Roger McFarland. He heard rumors of a large British Army massing for invasion of the area west of where he lived. After George Washington and his ragtag troops had been defeated at Fort Necessity and sent off like a dog with his tail between his legs by the French and their Indian allies, Lightfoot had been expecting this. He could see the interests of the French and English colliding. The native peoples would be in the middle and used by both sides. The Indians had their own interests, too. At this time, they favored the French. They were less of a threat to their land and way of life, but still the French were a threat. After French forces pushed the English traders out of the Ohio and the colonial forces under Washington back to Wills Creek, most western Indians sided with the French. They felt the English had no stomach for a fight and scornfully referred to them as "old women." And now in Winchester, Virginia he saw many Redcoats. He passed some of them as he traveled to town. Their bright uniforms stood out against the forest. They had horses, wagons for supplies, cannons, and many foot soldiers. Many were sick from the march already. The mosquitoes, chiggers, and ticks added to their woes. And the rattlesnakes had been a big problem. The soldiers seemed very afraid of "ye serpent with ye rattle tail." There had been a number of bites. Several men died. Still there were many, many soldiers. And many more still to join them at Wills Creek. He knew the stream by its Indian name, Cohongaronto. There Caiuctucuc, or old Will as the English knew the friendly Indian, had lived. On a hill overlooking the stream where it intersected the larger Potomac River, the English were building a formidable fort. It would be in the colony of Maryland across the river from the older and smaller blockhouse fortification, Fort Ohio, built by the Ohio Company in Virginia. This was, and would be, one of the main routes Virginia interests would use to reach the western parts of the colony. Virginia land claims went all the way to the Mississippi, some said all the way to the Pacific. Frontiersman Christopher Gist had twice been sent west to the Ohio River Valley to support claims and report on the vast, unknown area. The French also claimed the Ohio and west. There would be trouble Lightfoot knew. Various other tribes of Indians lived there and considered it theirs also.

Roger lived on a homestead near the blockhouse built on Mister Frank's farm, hence the name, Franksfort, or Frankfort as it was usually shortened. Before that, the area had been known as Franksford. The ford through Patterson Creek was near the Frank's family farm. Roger lived with his sister and her husband. Several other homes from neighboring homesteads were built near the blockhouse for protection from Indians if needed, but things had been fairly peacefully up until recently. Roger spent most of his time in the wood. That is where Lightfoot had surprised him and met him some years ago. Lightfoot would secretly shadow him home for his own safety. He was becoming a man of the woods, but he still had much to learn.

Groups of soldiers and supplies had been leaving the camp at Winchester almost daily. Roger got his needed goods and also left. The rugged road had been beaten down by troops. Lightfoot watched when Roger met the two Redcoats along the road. One appeared to be ill and the other had been attending to him. The three men now traveled together and Lightfoot followed. He wondered what the two Redcoats were doing apart from their unit. They did not act like deserters. The ill one probably had not been able to keep up with the army and the other Brit had remained with him to help. They continued on the beaten road until they reached the Little Cacapon River. There the beaten trail turned north to follow the river. Lightfoot knew the area well. The main body would follow the old Indian trail to the Potomac River. They could ford it at several spots. From there they would follow a trail little more than an animal path roughly paralleling the river to Wills Creek. It would be a long and hard journey for the men and supplies. Lightfoot watched the three cross the Little Cacapon and head up the hill on the other side. It was not much of a trail, but it led to the place where Roger lived. And, Lightfoot reasoned, Roger was taking the soldiers to Wills Creek by this way. It would be quicker than the other but more dangerous. He had already killed two Shawnee Indians watching the troops. He continued to follow, but less discretely. He wanted the young friend to know of his pursuing, but he would only leave the suggestion in Roger's mind of his presence. The soldiers seem to be traveling better, but he could tell they were not enjoying their time in the woods. The chiggers were eating them alive. They scratched almost constantly.

Soon they would be near the healing springs and stop there to refresh themselves. There Lightfoot would surprise them. He could see their faces now and laughed within himself.

He followed the main path till he came to the side trail that led to the springs. It would not be far. Lightfoot crept stealthily up the gentle rise. At the top, he lay on his stomach and looked through low branches and tree leaves. There in the healing springs, a neutral place where various tribes could gather at peace, were three naked and pale white men. Their cloths were laid to the side along with their weapons, too far to reach if they were ambushed. The men were enjoying the soothing waters and talking among themselves.

Like a phantom, Lightfoot emerged from the forest and stooped at the edge of the water. He glared at the naked men. The two British soldiers stopped talking and froze with fear. They were exposed and vulnerable. Roger looked up at Lightfoot. He said, "Oh, hello, I've been expecting you. Gentlemen, I would like you to meet my brother-in-law, Lightfoot."

With that, Lightfoot grinned and said, "You are getting better. You may make a woodsman yet."

"What are you waiting for?" Roger asked. "Come on in. The water feels great."

With that, Lightfoot stripped off his clothing and walked into the water. "And who are your friends?" he asked Roger.

Roger pointed to the first. "This is John De Fayre and that's Caleb Campbell. They are my friends. I'm taking them to the new fort on Wills Creek."

The two men looked at Lightfoot suspiciously and with some fear. Lightfoot smiled, "Any friend of Roger is a friend of mine. We will see you get there."

This was the first of several times the soldiers would see Lightfoot on their journey west to engage the enemy. Each time they would grow more thankful he was their friend.

Chapter 20

The men enjoyed the cool, regenerating waters of the spring. Periodically, Lightfoot would leave the waters. He was naked, but this did not bother him. As a child with the Monongahela tribe, he had worn no clothing, except in winter. Many in the tribe also "dressed" like this. The Tuscarora Indians had worn a little more but not much. Only when Lightfoot knew he would be around whites did he wear more than a breechcloth, legging, and moccasins. Now his pants and shoes lay on the bank. He looked carefully around the woods about the spring. He listened closely. All seemed in order, but the old rules seemed to be dying out. They were probably safe at this place the tribes considered sacred. The Great Spirit had given these healing waters to all His people. It was taboo to shed blood here, but things could happen. He skinned the dead animal, a raccoon, he had killed earlier. Lightfoot cut it up and put it over the fire to cook. Roger left the water and got a pot from his sack. He filled it with water, put some tobacco in the liquid, and set the pot on some rocks by the fire to heat. They then went back into the cleansing waters. The two soldiers were somewhat embarrassed at the comfort the other two men had in their bare skins but said nothing. Like good soldiers, they realized the two had superior knowledge of conditions here. They would watch. They would study and they would learn.

Lightfoot got out of the water. He looked at the men and said, "It is time, come."

Roger left the water first followed by the other two. He looked at the steeping water. Carefully he put his finger near the water. It was warm, not too hot. Then he cupped the brown fluid in his hand and rubbed it over his naked body. Lightfoot did the same. The two soldiers looked at each other uneasily. Roger smiled and said, "Do you want to get rid of those bugs that have been eatin' you up?"

The soldiers nodded yes. Roger said, "This stuff will kill them and keep them off of you."

Hearing that, they eagerly rubbed the liquid all over their bodies. They left no part untreated. The two frontiersmen laughed as they did. They knew the discomfort the bugs could do to a man. After they were dry, they dressed. Lightfoot checked on the meat. It was done, a little too done, but the men ate hungrily. John asked as he looked at the animal skin lying nearby, "What kind of animal is this?"

"Raccoon," Lightfoot replied, "but most people 'round here we just call it a 'coon'. 'Round here, if it moves or crawls, we eat it."

John and Caleb expressed mild surprise, but the warm meat was welcomed by their empty stomachs. After being left behind by the army, they had eaten nothing 'till Roger found them and shared his corn meal and maple sugar with them. Lightfoot walked around the pool to some cattails. He dug some out of the mire and cut some tender shoots. He washed the roots off, stripped the outer layer of both, washed them again, and gave this to the other men. Roger ate these without hesitation. The two soldiers followed his example. The roots and stems were good. Lightfoot smiled and said to them, "If you can ever find cattails, you will never go hungry. The soldiers nodded their approval. They were learning how to survive in this new land.

Late that afternoon, they passed the Edward's homestead. The Edwards and some neighbors were building a blockhouse on his property. They had heard the rumors of trouble and were preparing defense if needed. The four travelers proceeded on westward till nearly dark. The men chose a good place to lie down for the night. The weather was dry, but seasonally warm. Lightfoot as always was alert to the sounds of the forest. He showed no alarm. The three others picked up his cue and followed his example.

They traveled all the next day. Early in the morning, Lightfoot stopped and examined a broken twig and some moccasin marks. He looked intensely at the area before muttering, "Black Wolf."

This got Roger's attention. The soldiers looked at each other. Caleb asked, "Who's Black Wolf?"

"One very bad Shawnee Indian. He's smart and also very cruel," replied Roger. "He's a good one to avoid if you can."

They saw no more signs of the Indians that day, but they traveled ever vigilant. That night, the men camped by the South Branch River. They had no fire so as not to bring notice to themselves. After an uneasy night, they ate quickly and crossed the river at a ford. They traveled without much talk. By midday they were on top of Middle Ridge and would be at the home of Roger soon. The men continued without haste down the twisting hollow on the old trail that would get them to Frankfort. They would make it there by supper time if all went well. The four men crossed the shallow stream know as a 'run' numerous times. All were on guard for trouble. Lightfoot as usual was listening and looking for anything that would betray the presence of Indians.

The men moved on now eagerly but quietly. Lightfoot raised his hand and the party of four stopped. They stood there silently, listening, not moving. Lightfoot was looking intensely at something in the woods. Carefully and slowly he raised his gun to his shoulder, aimed, and fired. With Lightfoot in the lead, the men ran in the direction he had fired. There was blood on the ground. They followed it cautiously to a thicket. In the underbrush laid a dead deer. All would eat well tonight. Roger cut down a slender sapling. He tied the deer's legs and slipped the wooden pole through the legs. He signaled for the two

Redcoats to carry this. They put the poles on their shoulders and proceeded on, with Lightfoot in front and Roger guarding the rear. They had food, but the shot had alerted anyone near of their presence.

Soon they were in flat land, the fertile, bottomland along the stream known as Patterson Creek. A cabin came into view, but they found it deserted. The people had left in a hurry, so they continued on. At a distance, the cabins and blockhouse of Frankfort appeared in front of them. Menacing dogs started howling. They could make out people with guns looking in their directions. The dogs came running toward them growling viciously. Lightfoot yelled at them and their demeanor changed. Soon they were at his feet, wagging their tails, and yelping happily. Lightfoot reached down and rubbed the lead dog behind his ears and stroked his furry head. The dog left to sniff the first Red Coat. Lightfoot was now surrounded by dogs begging for attention. He rubbed all of them on their heads, necks, and backs. One by one they followed the lead dog, to sniff the soldiers, and then they turned their attention to the deer. They barked happily. The dogs would eat well tonight. Next, the pack checked out the second soldier and finally ran to Roger, who like Lightfoot, rubbed their heads and backs with vigor. The whole procession now headed toward the blockhouse and cabins. The people came running to them. All were armed.

"Lightfoot, Roger," a woman said, "We heard the shot and thought you were Indians." She looked at the dangling deer. "Now I know why we heard the shot."

Lightfoot smiled. "We will eat good tonight. I know about the Indians. Black Wolf and some others are passing through. I saw their tracks."

"Black Wolf," she said. "That can only mean trouble. How did you know it was him?"

Lightfoot responded, "The Indian's tracks were made by a man who's left foot is slightly pigeon toed. That's Black Wolf for sure."

She drew closer and kissed him. Lightfoot had married Beka about one year after her first husband, Reese, had died from the fever. Reese had cleared the land and built the cabin. Shortly after finishing it, he got sick and died. He was buried on the hill to the east of the little settlement. Beka had leased the cleared land to neighbors. They paid with a share of the crops. After marrying Lightfoot, she had continued this. Lightfoot was a man at home in the forest. He was no farmer.

In all, there were about eight armed men and women with her. One was a traveler. "Reverend Haskell! So good to see you," Lightfoot said.

"And you, too," the preacher replied. "I see you found some friends." He pointed to the Red Coats.

"Yes, they got separated from their group and we're taking them to Fort Cumberland."

"Not tomorrow," the preacher responded. "It's the Sabbath, our day of rest. You look like you all need it. And I'm not gonna miss a chance for some preachin' with all you'll here."

"So it will be. So it will be," said Lightfoot.

Lightfoot always liked to hear the preacher. He reminded him of his mother. He still did not understand the story of Jesus, the man who sacrificed Himself for us. This concept was foreign to a man raised as an Indian. They just did not do this. It was every man for himself, but he still liked the preacher. He was a good man.

The two Redcoats were made welcome. The men set to cutting up the deer. They skinned the buck and prepared the hide. The deer was quartered and the sections cut into smaller usable pieces. Those not to be used immediately were salted. The scraps were thrown to the awaiting hungry dogs. They wolfed the pieces down and eagerly but patiently waited for more. After a filling supper, the people sat around and talked about the sightings of Indians and other events in the settlement. A place for all to sleep was found in the crowded cabin. The still night was broken by the sounds of people snoring.

The next morning, Caleb was ill. As the day went by, he grew sicker. He could not keep fluids in his body. He had the trots, diarrhea. Beka put chamomile in some water for tea. The sick man drank it. It seemed to calm his stomach and bowels, but he was weak. A little after mid-morning, everyone gathered for Reverend Haskell's preaching. He had not been around lately and would not be by this way for some time, so he spoke long as was the frontier custom. All had their guns in case the Indians attacked. A sentry sat of the roof as a lookout as one had last night. John sat next to Beka and listened intensely. After about two hours of preaching, his stomach began to growl. Beka looked at him and smiled. She reached into her Bible and pulled out some dried plant leaves. "Chew these," she said.

John did and it quieted his complaining stomach. About half way through the services, Caleb got up and left swiftly. The diarrhea was back. He spent most of the day in the outhouse.

After services, everyone ate outdoors on one of the porches of nearby homes. Roger asked Lightfoot how he liked the sermon as they ate. He said he always liked to hear Reverend Haskell's preaching and teaching, but he still did not understand how Jesus would let himself die like that on the cross without a fight. He had never seen anyone do that in his life or heard of anyone who had done that. Roger told him, Jesus did it because of His love for us. Lightfoot looked unconvinced. John said it reminded him of the preachers in Ireland. It had been a long time since he had been to church. Caleb ate very little. John asked him how he was. "The bloody flux," he replied. "I think I have the bloody flux."

John's heart sank. The bloody flux had killed more soldiers than battle. Beka gave him more chamomile tea, but it did little good.

Aside from necessary chores, today everyone rested. It was much needed. The next morning, the day they had planned to continue on to Fort Cumberland, Caleb was too sick to travel. Tuesday showed no improvement, nor Wednesday, nor Thursday.

On Monday, after finding Caleb too sick to travel, Lightfoot lead the men into the forest to hunt. Beka found Reese's clothes and gave them to John to wear while he was in the woods. He liked the feel of the frontier garb, especially the soft moccasins. The clothes fit well. John and Reese had been about the same size. While in the woods, Lightfoot and Roger patiently and carefully taught John the ways of the frontiersmen. He absorbed the new knowledge like a sponge picked up water. He was a fast learner. John had realized his survival in this strange new land may depend on his ability to adapt. Each day that Caleb was too sick to travel, the men went to the woods. Lightfoot showed him how to track and listen to the sounds of the forest to read it. He gave him tips on shooting and showed him edible plants.

By Friday, Caleb looked like he was at death's door. Beka had been doctoring him with a mixture of opium, honey, licorice, and camphor, but it had done little good. The opium relieved the pain, but the flux remained. There was only one thing left to try in her frontier medicine, ipecacuanha. If this did not work, she feared for the young man's life. After she gave it to him, he vomited, as all do. Now it was wait and see. Friday showed little to no improvement. By Saturday, he was slightly better. The next day he showed more progress. By Monday, he was on the mend. By Wednesday, he looked his old self, but he was still weak. Daily, as they waited for Caleb's condition to improve, the three men took to the woods. John was feeling much more at home in the wilderness forest. Roger and Lightfoot both noted his rapid progress. It was now mid-May. The two frontiersmen and two soldiers left early Monday for Fort Cumberland. Caleb was still a little weak, but well enough to travel.

The men quickly traveled the old Indian trail that led to the gap in Knobley Mountain, commonly called Short Gap. They moved at a rapid pace through the gap and down the steep west slope. Within minutes, they were at the Potomac. In the shade of huge silver maples and sycamores they rested. John looked back from the direction they had come. He wanted to memorize just how the gap and the neighboring mountains looked. Someday he may need to retrace his steps and he wanted to know how. They forded the river. The water was cool and clear. Now they were in the colony of Maryland. The men followed the river the remaining miles to Wills Creek. Up the hill, they walked to the gate at the fort. There they were stopped by two sentinels. Because of their late arrivals, the sentinels took John and Caleb as returning deserters. Lightfoot and Roger tried to persuade them otherwise, but they would not listen. The sentinels tried to manhandle the two Redcoats, but were knocked to the ground by the frontiersmen. Quickly they were on top of the sentinels and had knives to their throats.

Redcoats came running, but stopped when they saw the situation. The tumult drew the attention of the two men in the tent. Out stepped General Edward Braddock, commander of the British forces and his volunteer aide, George Washington.

"What's going on?" demanded the General.

"Colonials have attacked our troops, Sir," came the reply.

"Preposterous," roared General Braddock.

George Washington looked at the situation. He recognized the one man, Lightfoot. "General," he said, "that's the man I was telling you about. That's Lightfoot."

The General's face softened. "Lightfoot," he said, "Get them all to my tent as soon as you can untangle them."

He went into his tent. Washington walked swiftly to the altercation. When he got there he called out, "Lightfoot, this is Colonel George Washington. The General requests your presence in his tent as soon as convenient."

Lightfoot shifted his eyes to the Colonel. He looked at the man he held down. He said to him, "No one questions my honesty and lives. But as a favor to Colonel Washington and your General, I give you your life."

With that, Lightfoot took his knife from the Redcoat's throat. A small trickle of blood ran down his throat from the small wound where Lightfoot had nicked him. Lightfoot wiped the blood from his knife and placed it in the sleeve. He stood up, looked down at the frightened man and stretched out his hand, "Come, now we are friends. Let us speak of this no more."

The startled man took the hand that a moment before held a knife meant to kill him. Lightfoot pulled him to his feet and smiled. Then he patted him on his back. The sentry smiled somewhat sheepishly. He was lucky to be alive. Roger had duplicated the actions of Lightfoot with the other soldier. He, too, had a relieved look on his face.

"Come," Colonel Washington said. "The General waits."

The five men walked across the grounds to the General's tent. It seemed every eye in the fort was upon them. They entered the tent and found the General seated. He spoke, "Mr. Lightfoot, Colonel Washington has told me much about you. He told me you were a ranger who could fight like ten men. I see this is true. Where have you been? You have been expected for two weeks."

"This young soldier," he said and pointed to Caleb, "was with us. He had the bloody flux and was too weak to travel. We could not leave him behind. We are here now and at you service."

"Good," the General said. "Good, I need scouts. I have only a few Indians now with us."

Colonel Washington grimaced. General Braddock was not much of a diplomat. It had been said of him by Governor Dimwiddle that he would just as soon fight the Colonials as the French. And his decision to send the Indian women home had unforeseen consequences. True they had been trading "favors" with Braddock's woman-starved troops, but when they left, so did most of the braves. There were only eight that remained. "And," the General continued smiling, "please don't kill any of my men. I need them all for battle."

Lightfoot looked at General Braddock. He smiled, "I like you, General. You have courage. May the Great Spirit give you wisdom in the days ahead. You will need it."

Some of the smile left General Braddock's face. "Yes," he said, "may God smile on this undertaking."

Washington added, "God rules in the affairs of man. May he grant us good fortune."

In his mind, Washington wondered. He had seen very little of a Godly nature about the General. He was vile at times and self-centered. His troops seemed to fear him more than the French and the Indians. He would meed out severe punishment for men with the coolness of a snake.

General Braddock looked at his men. "You two are to report to your commander, Sir Peter Halkett. If he has any questions on your return, inform him to contact me. You were away because of illness, understood?"

The two Redcoats tightened up and said sharply, "Yes Sir," in unison.

"Dismissed," General Braddock said. "Colonel Washington, show these men to their quarters. We have much to do before we travel, but it needs to be soon. The days are passing quickly and we have much to do before taking winter quarters."

The men left the tent. The Redcoats went to find their group, the 44th Regiment. Colonel Washington, Braddock's aide, took the two frontier men to their quarters. General Braddock sat alone in his tent thinking. *Would they be able to pull this complex operation off? The Colonial governments had promised much and delivered little in supplies and men. If Benjamin Franklin had not secured the wagons and horses, the mission would have failed here. The distance he had been told in England between his present position and the French fort at the forks of the Ohio was not fifteen miles, but one hundred fifty miles, ten times as far. A road must be cut through a mountainous wilderness. The King was counting on him. Surely he would be knighted if he could pull this off. The French had too few men and he did not believe the savages to be any match to his trained and disciplined troops. They would run when they saw his overwhelming forces. He would be dancing with the ladies of Philadelphia before the first snowfall. Perhaps if all went well, perhaps. Time would tell. Time would tell, but now he had much to do before he would lead his troops out of this protected encampment.*

Chapter 21

On the morning of June 7, 1755 the British 44th Foot Regiment left Fort Cumberland. John DeFayre and Caleb Campbell were with them. Wood cutters and scouts left days before to prepare the twelve foot wide road that must be built through the wilderness for the army. They followed the old Indian path that Delaware Indian Chief Nemacolin and Thomas Cresap had supervised improvements on at the behest of Christopher Gist of the Ohio Company earlier in 1749 and 1750. George Washington and his men widened it to six feet in 1754 on his way before his encounter with the French and their Indian allies at the hastily built Fort Necessity.

Today Interstate 68 in Maryland roughly follows the original trail as far as the Youghiogheny River.

The construction of the road through the frontier by the colonials and Redcoats was very slow and difficult. Mountains and rocky ridges had to be crossed. Ravines must be filled. Streams must be forded or bridged where possible. Thick marshes were in the way and of course, the ever present virgin forest with its huge trees challenged the effort.

The weather was unseasonably hot and dry. This helped the British forces but not the French. Reinforcements for Fort Duquesne had been slow in arriving, if they did at all. The waters in the streams the French depended upon for portage from the Great Lakes and Canada were very low. Even canoes needed to be carried in many places. Supplies only arrived with great effort. Reports of Braddock's great army made the Indians wonder at the wisdom of attacks on such a large force with the

French, but General Braddock knew little of this. He believed he had overwhelming forces that would be no match for the French.

He scorned the Colonial forces behind their backs and his visual contempt for them caused all but eight of his Indian scouts to desert his troops. He believed his well-trained British forces would probably scare the French forces and they would leave without a fight. His total forces consisted of 1350 Regulars, 500 colonials, and 50 seamen. He had cannons and horse drawn wagons with supplies. A young man named Daniel Boone was one of the colonial wagoners as was Daniel Morgan who would later become a famous Patriot commander during the American Revolution. On the British side, a young Scot named Hugh Mercer marched as a Redcoat. Two decades later, he would fight alongside George Washington at the Battle of Princeton during the war for independence.

Progress was slow, three to four miles a day. Underfed and overworked horses died pulling the heavy loads. Many men were sick with dysentery and the bloody flux. Some died. Indians picked off stragglers and those who wandered into the woods. Among the Indians was an Ottawa warrior named Pontiac who years later would lead a bloody war against the Whites. That war would bear his name. The 'lucky' soldiers caught by the Indians returned scalped and mutilated. Some victims were never found.

The Indians deliberately left others for the troops to discover. Some had been dismembered. The Indians delighted in putting the severed heads of the British soldiers on pikes. Their tall, red conical hats were placed on the lifeless heads with two open, unseeing eyes. None of this was good for the morale of the troops, especially the British. The Colonials goaded the British with tales of what they had seen or heard of the cruelties of the Indians. Still, they continued westward slowly but steadily toward the forks of the Ohio. General Braddock was concerned about the slow progress. There was still a grand plan to complete before winter quarters and the days were passing too quickly. He had expected losses of men and equipment. So far, they were in acceptable limits.

Rumors spread like wildfire among the troops. The thin line through the forest stretched for three or four miles in length. Many men fell ill, mostly dysentery, including Colonial Washington who rode like cargo in a wagon with other sick men and supplies.

The foot soldiers marched on westward. It could be mind numbing. Occasionally a man would trip over a root or stump and fall. The others would help pick up the cursing man. The sight of a snake of any kind sent the men scurrying. Regularly, the war whoops of the Indians were heard menacingly from the thick underbrush surrounding the newly cut road. It sent chills down the backs of the troops not used to this type of warfare. In Europe, armies battled in formation in wide-open space. How would the French and Indians fight here, from behind trees and rocks? John DeFayre wondered if General Braddock had considered this, or was he so confident, perhaps over confident of the superiority of the British forces, that he was self-blinded. If something did go wrong, he knew for sure the English Commanders would place the blame on the Irish soldiers. That was how it always was. They got the glory. We got the blame.

John thought of the stories his mother had told him of the history of the Scots. Originally from Ireland, the tribe had crossed the narrow sea and settled in the land to the east. There they united the other local tribes and gave the land their name, Scotland, Land of the Scots. The English had invaded and cruelly conquered them. They had then encouraged some of the Scots to return to Ulster or Northern Ireland. There the English pitted them against the Irish and took back, by deceit, the land the Scots had been given in Ireland. There was no future for him there. He had not wanted to be a British soldier, but when he found out they needed men for an army in the New World, he jumped at the chance. He had a free ticket across the sea and perhaps a new start in the New World. The voyage across the Atlantic was long, cold, and horrible in the cramped ship. John was seasick most of the way. It left him weak, but saved him a terrible fate. If he had been well, he would have jumped ship. Men did and were caught. Punishment was two thousand lashes.

When a man passed out, a bucket of cold, salt water was thrown on his bare back to rouse him. When a man had enough and could take no more, the doctor watching stopped the punishment. The lashes were resumed the next day. It took three days for some men to receive their full punishment. John had been thankful afterward for his weak stomach. The time would come for him to leave. The opportunity would be there when conditions were right.

It had been a hard march. John, Caleb and two other Redcoats had marched four abreast, with men before and behind him. Haystack Mountain, just outside of Fort Cumberland, was just a teaser of the difficulties to come. Big Savage Mountain claimed more than its share of broken wagons and sick men. They had walked through the tall hemlock, climax forest, they called the Shadow of Death. Sunlight barely pierced the thick, high canopy of green. There was no underbrush, only fallen needles and small branches that blanketed the ground. An eerie silence filled the forest. No birds sang. As John marched, he remembered the words of his mother from the Psalms, "Ye, thought I walk through the valley of the shadow of death, I will fear no evil." He found comfort in those words. He could read the fear in many of the Redcoats around him. There was nothing in Europe like this. It was like being on another world with unseen dangers all around. The silence was deafening. Surely a monstrous evil would gobble them up here. Finally, they arrived at the other side unharmed, but it took a while for the men's hearts to stop their rapid beating.

Over the coming days, the army camped at Little Meadows and later Great Meadows. John saw Colonel Washington riding slowly through the grassy flat lands. He stopped here and there. He looked to the right and then to the left contemplating. Here a year ago, the French and Indians had defeated Washington and his Colonials on this very spot. Charred logs stuck out of the meadow. This was all that was left of Fort Necessity. The enemy had destroyed it. Many men had died here on this spot. Washington sat on his horse quietly with his head down. The reins of his horse were loose in his hand. The horse ate from the grasses in the meadow. Washington seemed to be in prayer. After a few minutes, he tightened the reins and jerked them to the side. The horse turned and horse and rider trotted off toward the officers tents.

The next day, John heard through army grapevine, that Colonel Washington was sick again. The troops continued ever onward to the French stronghold at the forks of the Ohio. The way west wore on the men, horses, and wagons. Progress was slow, too slow to suit General Braddock. This could threaten the second leg of the plan for the attack on French forces on the St. Laurence River and Canada. The season for the war campaign was shrinking. If something wasn't done, winter would come, and the army would have to take winters quarters without completing the campaign. On June 19, General Braddock called a war council with all his officers. What should they do to speed up the operation? Many suggestions were made. Colonel Washington proposed a "flying column." The main fighting force of 1300 soldiers would surge on the forks. Colonel Dunbar would bring the slow moving wagons loaded with supplies and sick men along later. Six hundred men would stay behind to guard and move the wagons and supplies. All agreed to this plan.

That day, as the army rested, Colonel Peter Halkett rode through camp looking for three men for a special task. The men were ordered to line up in formation. Colonel Halkett rode alone beside the column. He stopped next to John and Caleb's row. This row had only three men, not the normal four. The fourth man had gone to the sick wagon to see the doctor. The third man's name was Robert Matthews. He kept to himself. Few people knew much about him. "You men," said Colonel Halkett as he pointed to the three, "Come with me."

The colonel led them back to the supplies. There four heavily laden horses awaited them. All the horses had poles strapped to their sides with a sling behind. The pole ends dragged the ground. The first two slings had a six inch cannon, commonly known as a 6 pounder because of the 6 pound shot it used, on each. The second set had two wooden boxes lashed to the poles and sling.

"Each of you," the Colonel said, "is to lead a horse with his left hand and follow me. Carry your gun in your right hand." The Colonel took the reins of the first horse. The three soldiers each went to a horse and did the same.

"Forward," the colonel said and the men, horses, and their burdens began to move. They followed the new cut road for about 200 feet and then turned right. The horses and men soon were walking in a small stream. The rocks were slippery. They moved carefully and deliberately. Quickly they were in a deep ravine. It snaked back and forth blindly. After about a thousand feet of this, the ravine opened up. The men could hear the rapids of the Youghiogheny River but could not see them.

"Stop," the Colonel commanded. "Tie the horses."

The men were then ordered to dig a large hole eight feet deep near a walnut tree. A nearby spring flowed into the stream. The men took shovels and picks that were in a long muslin sack next to one cannon and began to dig. Progress was slow. The virgin Pennsylvania earth was hard and full of rocks and tree roots. The Colonel watched from his horse. The three men dug for one half hour. The hard-fought hole was about 4 feet deep. The Colonel got down from his horse, walked to the hole and looked down at the men. He took his coat off and said to them, "Gentlemen, this never happened."

He took the pick from one man, told all three to rest and jumped in the hole and began to dig. The soldiers were shocked. This could not be happening. Officers in the British army just did not do this. The Colonel noted the men's dismayed looks. He said, "Gentlemen, some day in the future my hope is the British military system will be more just. A soldier should be able to rise to be an officer if he had the ability. An officer should not have to be a nobleman, or buy his position." The soldiers stood open jawed. "Until that day comes," he said, "until that day comes..., well, we've got a hole to dig."

"Yes, sir," The soldiers said in unison.

"Not yes sir," the Colonel said, "Mr. Halkett."

"Yes, sir," the soldiers said again.

Colonel Halkett smiled. The British military system had burned into the men's heads how they were to address the officers. There was no further point trying to change it. The four men continued digging, two in the ever-deepening hole, and two shoveling the dirt out of the way. The two outside had some time to rest. When the two in the hole got tired, they switched out with the other two.

The hole reached the required depth, eight feet. They manhandled one cannon, then another into the hole, breech down, open end up. The cannons were about 6 feet long. They then filled the hole with dirt until only one foot of the muzzle end stuck out. The Colonel led one horse with the box on the sling up to the hole. The box has a lock on it. He opened it with a key. Inside were many small cloth sacks. "Men," he said, "take everything out and place it in the cannons."

The men did as told. John noted the little sacks were heavy, very heavy for their small size. Like a bolt of lightning streaks across the sky, it came to him. They were burying the payroll for the troops. They had been told at Fort Cumberland they would not get paid until after the campaign ended. The men grumbled about this turn of events, but what could they do? General Braddock must have reasoned this would discourage the men from deserting. Those that died from disease or battle wouldn't have to be paid. It would save the King money. Perhaps the General would keep some of the savings. On the other hand, what would the soldiers have done with the money in the wilderness? There was no place to spend their pay. Even the Indian women that caused so much trouble at Fort Cumberland with their "favors" to the troops wanted paid in trinkets and goods for their "services." The soldiers would just have to grumble and live with the unpopular decision. What else could they do?

The men emptied the box. All the heavy little bags dropped down the barrel of the cannon. One box filled one cannon nearly to the top. The second box was emptied into the other upturned cannon. Colonel Halkett pulled two round plugs, probably oak or some other hard native tree, from a sack his horse carried and drove them into the end of the cannons with the metal side of the pick. The four men filled in the hole with the remaining dirt. They tramped it down, than covered the fresh dug earth with rocks and leaves. The men looked at the spot. Their work was finished.

"Tell no one of what happened here today," commanded Colonel Halkett.

"Yes, sir, "all the men replied.

John wondered to himself if he meant the candidness of the Colonel or the burial, or both. He looked at the other two soldiers. *Did they know what had been done here today? How could they not know? But it was possible to miss the obvious, to not see the forest for all those trees.*

"Soldiers," Colonel Halkett said to the men, "if you know how to ride, get on the horses and let's travel."

John and the other two mounted the horses clumsily. The Colonel smiled at this. "I see you are experts at horsemanship," he said and chuckled. "You are safe. The horses are gentle and will follow my horse. When we get back out of this ravine, you will dismount and walk the last leg leading the horse back to camp. Understood?"

"Yes, sir," the soldier responded as one.

"And tell no one of what occurred here today, understood?"

Again the men replied, "Yes, sir."

Before long, they were back at camp. They returned the horses to the makeshift corral. It had been an interesting day, but John would mention the events of the day to no one, not even his friend Caleb. Tomorrow would be another day. *What would it hold? How would the events of today affect his life if at all?* Time would tell. Now it was time for some supper and afterward—sleep. Tomorrow would be another day. It would probably be another day of marching till he was ready to drop, but you never know. Time would tell.

Chapter 22

The next morning the flying column departed. Colonial Dunbar, already angry with his menial assignment as supplies coordinator, grew even madder. He had been left behind with the sick and the cargo. He had been struggling to keep up the whole time and now that battle was over.

The General left with the best horses, artillery, and men. He would get the glory of the victory, and he, Dunbar, would be forgotten by history. Braddock left him with the broken down nags that passed as horses in this God forsaken land. *How was he ever supposed to get this mountain of supplies and men to the forks of the Ohio?* He seethed with anger, but what could he do? He would proceed on the best he could. He was in the British Army and that's what was required of him.

Lightfoot was near the front of the flying column. His skills as a scout were needed there. Elite troops with horsemen and artillery followed. After that came the 800 soldiers. John was needed at the rear of this group. Robert Matthews and Caleb marched along his side to his right. The fourth man of the row had not returned. There were also some wagons carrying needed supplies including rum. The whiskey had run out and the soldiers complained bitterly over this. One carried trinkets and gifts to any Indians that would join them after the defeat of the French at the forks. Behind them were the same elements only in reverse. The flanks were covered by scouts and horsemen. Braddock traveled cautiously. He wanted no mistakes. The army proceeded on faster without the slow moving burdens now under the care and protection of Colonial Dunbar and his men. Among them was George Washington. He was again too sick and weak to ride his horse.

On June 28, the army was now thirty-five dangerous miles from the walls of Fort Duquesne at the forks of the Ohio. Indian scouts reported to General Braddock that reinforcements for the French were on the way. Because of this, the decision was made to continue on without haste and not wait for Colonial Dunbar who was getting further and further behind.

About one week later on July 8, Braddock's army camped just two miles from the Monongahela River. The troops were in good spirits. Oxen had arrived from Dunbar. Soon every soldier's belly was full of fresh beef, the first time in weeks. The march was near over. The skulking Indians, mosquito filled marshes, wood ticks and chiggers, and gut-rotting drinking water would be behind them. They could relax.

At Fort Duquesne, Captain Contrecoeur assessed his situation there. There was no way the dirt and wooden walls of the structure could withstand Braddock's artillery or his overwhelming number of troops. Reinforcements that had been sent for him had been diverted elsewhere as needed against the British grand plan of invasion of French claimed territory in North America. He would have to use whatever resources he had. What he did have was 500 French and Canadians skilled at frontier warfare and 1,000 Indians from many tribes whose support was wavering after seeing the vast British juggernaut coming. He had only two choices, surrender the fort with honors, or attack the flying column before it reached the ill-prepared fort. If he did the latter, he could expect no quarter. He chose the latter. The brilliant Captain Beaujeu, loved by the Indians like a father, would lead the attack.

Later that day, Braddock's army crossed the drought-lowered Monongahela River. They camped on the west side overnight under heavy guard. So far, they had met no resistance. Tomorrow they would be in possession of the near French fort. They would drink the French men's wine and sleep in his fort if all went as planned. What could possibly go wrong?

Chapter 23

On July 9 Captain Beaujeu woke early. Before dawn, he and his troops went to Mass and received communion from Father Denys. His troops, 250 French regulars and Canadians, all were dressed Indian style, naked to the waist and with a breechcloth and leggings, now waited patiently for their commander who was still with the Father. He emerged from the rough building and was also dressed Indian style. He wore a shiny, silver gorget on his chest. He led them to the main gate where a large crowd of Indians waited. He said, "I asked you before, are you coming with me?"

"No, father," they replied. "We will not march."

"Very well," he replied. "I shall attack."

He then looked at them scornfully and asked, "Will you let your father go alone?"

This chastisement was too much for the Indian's pride as fighting men. 600 warriors were now clamoring for guns and ammo. These were quickly distributed. The Indians began to put on war paint and then started to dance wildly. It was mid-morning before the howling mob of 900 whites and red men boiled out of the fort. By afternoon, they neared the Monongehela. At that point, they broke into a run. They wanted to catch the British before they crossed the river. Through the open forest before him, Beaujeu glimpsed something. Coming toward him was the high pointed hats and scarlet coats of the British. The British saw him at the same time. Quickly, Beaujeu had the French regulars halt. He signaled the Indians with his hat to go right and left to flank the enemy, which they did rapidly. A French volley was answered by the British, then a second and a third that put a bullet through the French commander's head. The Indians wavered at 'their father's' death. Captain Dumas, second in French command, quickly began giving orders and reassuring the Indians. The battlefield soon filled with a thick cloud of gun smoke. The British troops in the open forest were having a hard time finding targets in the smoke and their enemy hid behind the many large trees. They fell like autumn leaves in the wind. Colonial Gage tried to keep order and find targets without success. He gave the order to retreat, but had to stop almost immediately. The troops behind him were advancing into the retreating men! Confusion became chaos and the Indian's loud screams added more to the bedlam. Even in the smoke, the red coats made easy targets for them.

John De Fayre had just crossed the river with his fellow soldiers when they heard shooting. It grew louder and closer. They officers ordered them forward quickly. General Braddock, followed by Colonial Washington, rode by swiftly on horses toward the front. All rushed forward only to be caught up in a tangled mass of soldiers. Men cried out in pain as they were shot. General Braddock tried to control and direct the confused mass, but met with little success. Soldiers shot fellow soldiers in the confusion. Redcoats killed Colonials that hid behind trees Indian style. The confusion and carnage continued for nearly two hours. John De Fayre watched in horror as men around him died. Caleb fell and died early with a shot through the chest. General Braddock continued to try to rally his panicked troops, but things only got worst. The last thing John remembered was seeing a riderless horse galloping from the smoke. It hit Robert Matthews and knocked him into John. Their heads collided and both went down motionless. The battle passed around them. General Braddock fell from his horse, shot through the arm and chest. Colonel Washington came to his aid. The General was seriously wounded. Without a leader, the army began to retreat. Washington ordered the necessary retreat and gathered Colonial soldiers he could find to guard the rear as the army fled.

John awakened in a daze to find someone pulling on him. It was Lightfoot. He had seen John lying on the ground and was checking to see if he was alive. "Get up. You must," he said, "if you want to live."

With effort John did get up and followed the other men retreating. Lightfoot and a number of other Colonial soldiers guarded them as they headed for the other side of the river. There they rested for a moment, but fearing pursuit, they hurried off down the newly cut wilderness road.

On the other side of the river, the Indians could not believe their fortune. Never had they seen so much spoil from a battle. Guns lay everywhere. There were hundreds of scalps to be had. They put the high hats of the British on their heads and began to take scalps and any treasures they could find among the dead. Occasionally, an Indian would let out a hideous whoop. Soon a tomahawk would finish off a wounded soldier. Bodies of men and horses laid everywhere.

An Indian worked his way through the fallen soldiers. He was looking for something special. He wanted to find someone living to mark for torture later at the fort, but all were too far-gone, so he kept looking. He rolled a bloody dead man off another. There he found a man unconscious. The man was Robert Matthews. He painted his face black, marking him for death by slow torture. He cut the clothes from the unconscious man and tied his hands behind his back. Then the Indian slapped the sleeping man hard across the face. Robert Matthews woke and saw a hard-faced Indian staring at him. The Indian's face had a large wine stain birthmark on it. Black Wolf spoke to him coldly. "You die slowly."

Black Wolf jerked him to his feet and led him away like a man leads a dog he hated. Robert was tied to a tree with a group of other naked captured soldiers, all with black faces. There were also five women tied and clothed just like the men.

Five hours later the prisoners were lead into Fort Duquesne. The Indians had found the British rum and were getting very drunk. They had lit torture fires. The women were taken off to a building. When they emerged, they all were clothed like Indian women. If lucky, they would be held for ransom. If not, they would be sold into slavery. The men would not be so lucky and Robert knew it. "Help me," he yelled to no one in particular. "Help me!"

Francois Geoffrey knew what would happen soon. The drunken Indians would torture the unfortunate men with fire. He had seen Indians kill men this way. Some men took three days to die.

"Help me," the tied young man continued. "Help me."

He caught the eye of the French man. "Help me, I can make you wealthy," he pleaded. "I know where the General's gold is. Help me."

Francois walked up to the tied man. "What did you say? You know where the General's gold is? What gold and where?"

Robert pleaded, "General Braddock's payroll. I know where it's buried, over on the river. I know where it is. It's a king's ransom and I will take you there, just help me."

Francois was interested. He went to the Indians to buy the young man. No, they said. He was marked for death. Again, Francois pleaded for the young man. No, they said harder and somewhat threateningly. Francois knew not to argue with drunken Indians. He left them with their rum.

Stealthily he worked his way back to the doomed man. "I cannot help you, more than this. I hope it is enough."

Francois slipped a small, sharp knife into the tied hands of the man and then slipped away. Robert feverously worked to cut the cords that bound him. He succeeded, but the Indians were now coming. He put his hands behind his back. When they got to Robert, he jumped and savagely struck them with the knife. He yelled wildly which startled the drunken men. He slashed and stabbed like a man who knew he was going to die. The Indians backed away. Robert walked to the biggest one, looked him eye to eye, than spat in the warrior's face. This was too much for the Indians. With tomahawks, they fell upon the white man. Soon he was dead, very dead. The Indians make sure of that.

Francois watched this all from a dark shadow nearby. *Pity*, he thought. He had not been able to save or get more information from the young man. His quick death was a blessing compared to the fates of the other men. But still he knew, somewhere to the east along a river was buried a fortune in gold. Perhaps someday he would find it. *Yes, someday, perhaps*, s*omeday*.

Chapter 24

Colonel George Washington accessed the retreating troops and supplies. Most of the officers were dead. He alone was unharmed even though two horses had been shot out from under him and his clothes had numerous bullet holes. General Braddock had died. He had said little in his last days. Washington had been at his side. "Who would have thought?" the General had murmured. "We shall better know how to deal with them next time." After this lament, the General breathed his last.

Out of his three companies of Virginia troops, only thirty men were still alive. With these men, the Colonel had guarded the retreating British army. He was disgusted with Colonel Dunbar, the now ranking British officer. Even though they still had more than 1,600 men and much supplies, Dunbar had chosen to run like a sheep chased by wolves back to Fort Cumberland. They had enough of everything needed to return and counter attack, but the coward Dunbar had burned all the supplies along the new road. The only good thing to come from this was there was now an overabundance of wagons to carry the wounded.

The retreat went rapidly back to Fort Cumberland. There had been next to no pursuit. Washington heard of only a few incidents. He reasoned the Indians were too busy celebrating. They would return to their villages with their spoils, scalps, and trinkets. Soon there would be trouble. Colonel Dunbar had decided to seek winters quarters in Philadelphia and it was only July! How would they defend the frontier against the Indians? The new road was now another burden. It led straight to the unprotected colonies of Pennsylvania, Maryland, and Virginia.

All three of their Governors had pleaded with the coward, but on August 2 he left, taking both British and Colonial forces with him. Within days, the French and Indians began their raids. Dawns were now filled with fear. This was the time they usually struck killing, burning, destroying, and scalping. Terror spread in every direction. The British had forgotten this part of their colonies. The British troops had been seen as their saviors, but now they were scorned and despised. The colonies would have to fend for themselves. Hundreds of settlers died horribly on lonely backwoods farms. Within sight of Fort Cumberland, a woman named Jane Fraser was abducted by the Indians and carried to Ohio. Eighteen months later, after escaping her captors, she found her way back. Her husband thought she was dead and had remarried. This scene happened many times on the frontier during these horrible times.

By the spring of 1756, the colonies began to take action though it was painfully slow. Governor Dinwiddie ordered Colonial Washington to oversee a chain of forts from the Potomac in the north to the New River in the south to protect the settlers. Pennsylvania followed a similar course. Four were built up the Patterson Creek Valley. Many more were built for protection on the South Branch and Cacapon Valley. Many settlers formed their own defense. Any cabin, mill, tavern, or other kind of building could become a makeshift fort in time of danger. Any backwoods farmer could become an Indian fighter and did.

One group of men worked the fields, while another group covered them and looked for Indians. During attacks, all fought. The women and children reloaded and primed the guns as needed. They often took over the men's position at the firing slot if he was killed or wounded. They also tended the wounded. Anything could be a weapon, an ax or mattock, even a kettle of boiling water would do. The Indians would rarely attack a well-prepared fort. Still, they were too far apart and often too thinly manned. Long stretches between them went unpatrolled.

Many died. In the lower Patterson Creek area alone, three whole families were murdered. There was just too much area, too few volunteers, too little clothing, food, arms, or money. Fortunately, for the settlers, the following winter was severe and the Indian threat diminished for a season.

In the year of 1757, things began to change. The frontiersman's defenses had stiffened.

The Virginians were able to make raids on the Indians. The hunters sometimes became the hunted.

Early that year, Colonel George Washington made his rounds to inspect the forts along Patterson Creek and later those along the South Branch drainage. Fort Sellers, near the mouth of Patterson Creek, he found understaffed, but in order. He passed numerous burned out homes and barns as he rode to the next fort, Frankfort. It was in order, but he had to reprimand his old friend, Captain Ashby, who commanded there. It seemed his wife had been causing some unspecified but disagreeable trouble. This had to stop or the colonel would replace the captain. While at the fort, Colonel Washington had a surprise. He chanced to meet two men he knew. One was Daniel Morgan whom he greeted warmly. Morgan had a bandaged face from a bullet wound he had received in an encounter with Indians near the Cacapon River. He would carry a scar as a reminder until his dying day.

The second man, Washington called aside out of hearing of the other troops. "I know who you are," he said to the startled man.

"You're John De Fayre. You should be with the British army, not here in this frontier stockade. Even with the beard and frontier clothing, I still know you. I never forget the eyes. They never change."

The man sunk back. The colonel knew he was a deserter from the British army. The colonel added, "Any friend of Lightfoot is a friend of mine. And I need good fighting men here. I've heard nothing but good reports about you, *Mister*

Phares. I see you have taken a new name. Your secret is safe with me. Dunbar and his cowards ran, but you chose to stay here with us and fight. Thank you and keep up the good work."

From then on John knew the secret of his past was safe. John, Lightfoot, and Roger remained at the fort throughout the next two years.

In 1758, Colonel Washington and his Virginia troops would join British General Forbes at Raytown, today known as Bedford, Pennsylvania. From there, 6,000 troops would head to Fort Duquesne and finally run the French from the Ohio River Valley forever. George Washington would again narrowly escape death in the thick fog along Loyalhanna Creek, this time from friendly fire. He commented later he was never more scared in his life than that day. General Forbes would die soon afterward from a chronic illness. After the defeat of the French at various battles on the frontier, the Indians drifted back to the west.

Peace came for a while, but some Indians still had hate in their heart and scores to settle. From his shelter above the Monongehela River, Black Wolf could think of only one thing, revenge. Lightfoot must die.

Chapter 25

In the year of 1759 Black Wolf and two other warriors traveled the hills and valleys of western Pennsylvania, Maryland, and the area that today is West Virginia. They were all that was left of his band of marauders. The others of his once proud group were lost in the war with the British and American forces. Few had died in the great battles. Most had been picked off one by one. He lost the majority while in the Patterson Creek Valley area and he believed this to be the work of one man, Lightfoot. His first braves died many moons ago. His men had been hunting near the blockhouse of Thomas Cresap not too far from the Potomac River. He remembered the tall gangly red-haired youth he saw there, young George Washington. He had tried to kill him several times over the years. The first time was at Fort Necessity. The second was when he was with Braddock. How his many bullets missed, he did not know. The third time was on the way from Fort Cumberland to Fort Ashby. He slipped like a ghost through their fingers on that foggy morning. The Great Spirit must have His hand of protection on him. Black Wolf had tried to kill Lightfoot with several shots at the battle where Braddock died, but Lightfoot had wounded him there with a shot that pierced his side. He wanted to wash his hands in Lightfoot's blood and soon he would.

For the most part, the three Indians kept a low profile. When they did contact the white eyes, they were peaceful. They sought only what they needed from the pale faces to survive and get them closer to their goal. They had a score to settle. They wanted to kill Lightfoot. Black Wolf hated him and had a plan for his death. How he longed for that day of sweet revenge. The men had scouted the Frankfort settlement with the fort commanded by Ashby. Black Wolf had a devious plan. It burned in his belly and he longed to fulfill it. It would give him great satisfaction.

The settlers had lowered their guard. The Indians had been driven west of the Ohio and were seeking peace, most but not all. The trio watched patently but anxiously the morning when Lightfoot and Roger left the cabin to go hunting. They watched as Lightfoot kissed his wife and two-year-old son good bye. Roger gave his sister and nephew big hugs before they left. The Indians only waited about five minutes before they struck. They kicked the door to the homestead open and entered. Beka went for a gun, but it was too late. A tomahawk to the head by Black Wolf ended her life quickly. That was part of the plan. Black Wolf grabbed the little boy and the two other Indians set fire to the house. They drug the dead woman outside. Then the trio went west toward the reedy field along where Patterson Creek and Turners Run came together. The reeds were thick and about four feet high. From there they would spring their trap.

Lightfoot and Roger were not far into the woods to the east of the settlement when they heard the bell, the alarm bell at the fort. They ran back to the fort. There, just outside the fort, was the cabin of Lightfoot and Roger in flames. The men ran over to the burning cabin. Other armed men of the village stood by. Lightfoot saw his wife dead. He looked at one of the men who said, "The Indians took your boy. There were three of them and one had a purple birthmark on his face."

"Black Wolf," Lightfoot and Roger said in unison.

They looked at each other. They knew what must be done. Mourning would have to wait. The child must be recovered. They knew Black Wolf wanted them dead. They were probably heading for a trap set by the Indians, but they had no choice if they wanted the boy. And Black Wolf was counting on this.

"We will go with you," a man in the crowd at the burning house said.

"No," said Lightfoot. "Black Wolf wants me and me alone. Others will die if they come. I must go alone."

"No," said Roger. "I will go with you."

Lightfoot looked at Roger and nodded his head. "Come, we must go, quickly."

The other men pointed in the direction the Indians had gone. They had made no effort to hide their tracks. They wanted to be followed. A trap had been set but where, how soon?

The men forded Patterson Creek. The water was knee deep and maybe forty feet across. The air was cool under the silver maple and sycamores trees by the water. Almost immediately, they were in the reeds and the trail ended. The Indians had gone to great effort to conceal their path. Lightfoot was in the lead. Roger traveled ten feet behind. Out of the thick reeds sprang two warriors who fell on their pursuers. Lightfoot had been expecting an ambush. The first attacker was met with a gun barrel that diverted his blow and then a gunstock to his head that killed him. Roger engaged the second attacker in a hand-to-hand struggle he knew only one would survive. The two men rolled in the reeds wrestling for an advantage.

Lightfoot turned to help Roger, but a little voice somewhere ahead called out, "Daddy."

Roger must win this on his own. He must save his son. Lightfoot rushed forward through the tall reeds. "Lightfoot," came a voice from behind him. "I have your son."

Lightfoot slowly turned back toward the voice. He saw the wine stain marked face of Black Wolf. "I have your son, Lightfoot, and I will kill him."

Black Wolf held a large carving knife to the neck of the boy. "I could kill him now, then you and I would fight to the death. Would you like that? Or I give you a second choice. You can let me kill you now, and I will let the child live. What do you think of that? I give you this choice today. Sacrifice yourself and the boy lives. Or he dies and then we fight. What is your choice?"

Lightfoot looked at the knife to the boy's throat. Surely the boy would die. Lightfoot asked Black Wolf, "Why should I believe you will let the boy live?"

Black Wolf gave a cruel smile. "Why? Why would I let him live? Because it will give me great satisfaction every day I live. I will raise him as my own son. He will grow up and kill many white men. And every day when I see him, I will remember how I killed your wife and bested you. That is why I will let him live. What do you say Lightfoot? What is your choice?"

Lightfoot looked at his son. He wanted him to live. Lightfoot tossed his gun into the reeds and looked at Black Wolf. He knew the Indian spoke the truth. "Let the boy live. I give you my life."

He turned and faced Black Wolf. The Indian smiled and lowered the boy into the reeds. He raised his gun to his shoulder and took aim at Lightfoot's head. How could he miss at this short range? A shot rang out, but it was Black Wolf that fell to the ground dead. Lightfoot turned to see Roger kneeling in the reeds. Roger had killed Black Wolf. Lightfoot picked up his son. He looked at the bloody body of Black Wolf. He then walked to Roger. "Are you all right? What happened to you?"

"The big Indian tried to kill me with his war club, but I managed to slip a knife between his ribs. He fell on me and I liked to never got his dead body off of me," Roger said. "I heard what you said to Black Wolf, how you were willing to sacrifice yourself for your son. That is what Beka and me have been trying to tell you about Jesus. He was willing to sacrifice himself so that we may live. That's the message of the Gospel."

Lightfoot's eyes widened. He nodded his head. "Now I understand."

Later that day, they buried Beka on the hill to the east of the fort. Recent graves marked the final resting spots of many homesteaders here in the Patterson Creek Valley. This had been the front line in the war with the French and Indians. Many had died here. Death was always near for the people here on the American Frontier. More would die before the conflict was finally over, but today two men and boy sat near the heaped up mound of a new grave.

Lightfoot looked at Roger. He said, "I have made my peace with Jesus. I just wish it hadn't taken this for me to see."

Roger nodded, "That is good to know."

"Just wish that Beka could know of this."

Roger smiled, "I think she does."

Lightfoot looked at him puzzled. "How could she know?"

"God's word tells us that when a lost soul is found, the angels dance and rejoice," Roger responded. "I think she will notice the commotion and ask what the celebration is about. She will know. She will know."

Lightfoot smiled, "That is good to know."

The two men sat silently there for a long time. The little boy had fallen asleep on the leaves and grass.

Finally, the men arose. Lightfoot put the sleeping boy on his shoulder and they walked to the fort. This would be their home tonight. Tomorrow was another day. The men would have to adjust to their new reality without Beka. Life would have to go on without her just as it would with everyone ever born. There is a season to be born and a season to die. Lightfoot was glad he was ready. He was now ready for the day he would die. He hoped that all could know this peace. Many times he would go to her grave and tell her this. He found peace when he talked with her. And he thought she knew.

Chapter 26

It was late afternoon when John first saw the weary travelers heading toward his cabin. The three came over the old Indian trail that ran past the burned out cabin of Mr. Dennison. Indians had killed the Dennison family in the war. John helped bury them. The road past the cabin continued up and over Middle Ridge and then to Winchester 40 miles further east. People were slowly returning to the frontier now that the Indians had been vanquished, but there was still a report now and then of sightings. The three travelers were a strange sight, the short, fat, bald man riding the horse and the two women walking behind. The man was well dressed for the frontier, as was the first woman. The second woman, with flaming red hair, wore tattered and well-worn clothing. Her hair had not seen a comb for days.

From his cabin porch, John watched as they got closer. Finally they arrived. The short, fat man looked down from atop his horse and said, "How do you do? My name is James Durham. This is my wife, Elizabeth." He pointed to the first woman, who nodded. "And this is my maid servant, Jenny."

He pointed to the second woman. She wearily looked at John. She was younger than John, he guessed by five to ten years. Even through the grime and dirt John could tell she was pretty, very pretty. A little soap and water was needed to improve her appearance. The other travelers needed it, too, but mostly Jenny. She looked tired. *Probably an overworked indentured servant*, John thought.

He was right. Durham asked if they could stay at the cabin for the night. He said the girl could sleep in the shed, but John insisted that all would stay in the cabin. John added salted pork to the beans cooking over the fire. He asked the trio to fetch water and milk from the spring house and pick some vegetables from the garden. James ordered the girl to the distant spring house. He and his wife picked some greens, onions, and radishes from the garden, but the wife did the majority of the work. The misses prepared the greens and onions and put them in the pot of water to cook over the fire in the hearth. John already had cornbread and a rhubarb cobbler made. Sometime later, Jenny appeared with a bucket of water in one hand and a smaller container of milk in the other. Jenny said nothing and set her burdens down. James fussed at Jenny, "Girl, can't you move any faster? I'm hungry, can't you see?" John poured some of the water Jenny had brought in the coffee pot and put it over the fire. When it was hot, he would throw in some coffee grounds.

Jenny said nothing and set her burdens down. James continued, "Don't stop now, lazy girl." Jenny cringed, but did as she was told. "These servants just ain't what they used to be. Treat them kindly and what gratitude do they show?" James said to John. James continued, "I bought her services down at Alexandria. She's mine for four years. She's been with me 6 months. You would think she'd know more by now. This world just ain't what it was when people knew their place and were thankful for it."

The supper was good. The beans with salt pork were tasty and the mixed greens hit the spot. The Englishman, Durham, dominated the conversation during the meal. It was mostly about how people needed to know their place, especially the poor. He bragged on how the English had conquered the world, especially the Irish. He couldn't understand how the brave English General Braddock had been defeated. It had to be the Colonials and Irish troops fault. John knew what happened. He kept his peace. This was too much for the quiet Jenny. She said, "The English butchered my people and took their land."

With that, James raised his hand to strike Jenny. John grabbed his arm and with authority said, "We'll have none of that in my house." Flustered by this James, retreated, "Sorry," he said. "Don't know what came over me."

John knew all too well the way the English had treated the Scots and the Irish. What Jenny said was true. John thought of how the English treated William Wallace. More recently, the Duke of Cumberland's troops slaughtered and raped their way across Scotland. He had no love for the English. They ate the rest of the meal in near silence. Occasionally someone would ask for something to be passed. When they were finished, John asked the women to clean up and James to come outside with him.

The men got up from the table and walked outside. When they were about 100 feet from the cabin, John stopped and the Englishman did, too. John looked at him sternly and said, "You are a guest in my house and I expect your best behavior."

"So, so, sorry," said James, "don't know what came over me. That wench has a tongue on her. Sometimes I wonder why I even bought her."

John looked at him and asked, "Would you sell her to me? I have no woman here and I need one." James looked a little surprised. Quickly his calculating mind thought. "Yes, if the price be right. She's a sturdy wench and hard-working, but oh, that tongue. Sometimes I've wanted to cut it out, but how would she eat?"

John ignored the question. He reached for the Englishman's hand and put a gold coin in it. Mr. Durham looked at it and smiled. He bit it with his teeth. It was soft and he smiled more. "Why that's the real thing. Where did you get this?"

John ignored that question, too, and placed another coin in his hand. The Englishman's smile grew larger. He said, "Now, I do own her for three and half more years."

John reached into his pocket for more coins. He placed four more in Mr. Durham's stubby hand. His smile grew larger "And she's a strong thing."

John looked at him and said, "But she has a surly tongue and can be insubordinate."

Mr. Durham replied, "Let's say she's spirited."

John put two more coins in the outstretched hand. The Englishman's smile grew still larger. John looked at him and said, "Tomorrow morning before dawn you and your wife will leave and never return. And you are not to tell Jenny, agreed?" James looked at the two additional gold coins John held between his fingers. "Agreed?" John asked again.

"Agreed," said Mr. Durham, "You drive a hard bargain. After tomorrow you will never see me again."

John had not driven a hard bargain. He had greatly overpaid, but he wanted Jenny. The fat man put the ten coins in a small cloth sack with a drawstring. John pointed out the corners of his property from the high point where the cabin sat. Durham pulled Jenny's indentureship paper from his breast pocket. He printed on it, "I, James Durham, on June 20, 1759 in the year of our Lord, do sell the indentureship of my servant, Jenny Kelly to John Phares." Then he signed his name and also wrote "Paid in full." He gave the paper to John. "Well, I hope you enjoy her services as much as I did," James Durham said in a joking but a little sarcastic way.

They walked back to the house. It was getting dark. They went in the house now lit by the fire in the hearth. John told Jenny she was to sleep up in the loft in the hay. He and the Durhams would sleep on the hay mattresses on the floor. She indicated she understood and shortly afterward climbed the ladder to the loft. The rest of the people there soon were in bed and asleep quickly, except for John. He was thinking of what to say to Jenny tomorrow after the Durhams were gone. Mr. Durham was snoring loudly. Eventually John drifted off to sleep.

The night passed quickly. John heard the Durhams stirring, getting up and dressing. He saw John and whispered, "We're leaving, good luck to you and your prize."

John followed them out the door which he closed gently. The sky on the horizon showed a glimmer of light. The Durhams left quickly. John sat on the bench on the porch and watched the sun rise. The cabin faced the east. John loved this time of the day. Each day brought new hope. When it was bright enough to see he went to the chicken coop for eggs. He found four the hens had laid and put them in a small basket he had. He carried these to the cabin and went inside. Jenny was up. She was carving ham off the bone. She placed the slices on a plate. John went to the fire. He noted Jenny had just put the coffee left over from last night on the fire to heat. It was not boiling, but the pot of water next to it was. John carefully placed the eggs into the boiling water. He turned to the young woman. "Jenny we need to talk, take a seat," John said. She sat down on the bench across from the table from John. "Jenny, the Durhams are gone," John said. "Mr. Durham sold your services to me last night." And he laid the legal paper on the table.

Jenny looked stunned. Then she grabbed the butcher knife she had used for carving the ham and rose from her seat. She looked at John with fear and anger. "John Phares," she said sternly as she pointed the knife in his direction, "I'll wash your clothes, I'll clean your house, I'll cook your food, but I WILL NOT BE YOUR WHORE!!!"

John had expected her to be surprised, but not this. He could see she had taken a defensive position. He looked her in the eyes. "Jenny Kelly," he calmly said. "You will wash my clothes, clean my house, and cook my food, but I have never wanted, nor needed the services of a whore."

Jenny's face looked like it could crack. She sat down and laid the knife on the table. She buried her face in her hands and began to cry. All John could see was her hands and tangled red hair. Slowly he moved the knife away. "Jenny," he said, but she didn't notice. "Jenny," he said again, but she continued to cry vehemently.

He got up from the table, left the house, and sat in the handmade chair on the porch. The sun was now fully over Middle Ridge. He sat there thinking. Ten minutes passed. The door opened and out came Jenny. She carried a plate of food and a cup with steaming coffee. "Sir," she said. This is for you. I am sorry I spoke to you in such a manner. I had no right. I ask your forgiveness."

John took the plate and cup. He sat it on the porch bench. "It's okay, Jenny," he said. "It's okay, get yourself something to eat."

She went in the cabin and quickly returned with her food. John told her to take a seat and they ate together. This would be the first of many mornings they spent this way.

* * * *

Two weeks later

The sun was its zenith that warm day when the traveler from the west stopped at John's cabin. His horse and the one that followed were piled high with furs. Jenny sat on the porch shelling peas. "Hello," said John to the fur trader. "How are you and where have you come from?"

"I am as well as can be expected," he replied. "I just came from the forks of the Ohio."

"How are things there, now that the French are gone?" John asked. "I hear the Indians have switched sides."

"The British and Colonial forces are busy building a substantial fort at the forks," he said. "They're calling it Fort Pitt in honor of William Pitt, the Prime Minister. Most of the Indians are now cooperating with the British, not the French, but not all. I chanced upon a grisly sight near Great Meadow. The Indians, probably Huron or Ottawa, left a dead man tied to a tree, by the trail for all to see," he said. "He was missing a leg. It looked to me that they had eaten it while he watched. They had cauterized the wound from the missing leg with fire. I believe, after eating the leg, they cut his tongue out, and then blinded him. After that, they scalped him and sank a tomahawk in his head to kill him finally."

"What did he look like?" John asked.

"He was short and stout, probably bald," the fur trader replied. Jenny looked up from her labors, but said nothing. "From the clothing they left, I'd say he was an Englishman."

John asked, "Was there any evidence of a woman with him?"

"Yes, I saw what looked like part of a torn dress on a tree shard," he replied. "I suspect they are taking her back to their village, if they don't kill her on the way. If they are pursued and she is too slow, they will kill her. Or they may get hungry. If she made it to their village, she could be adopted into the tribe, used as a slave, or sold to the French."

"The dead man sounds like the traveler who went through here about a week ago with his wife," John said. "That's too bad."

The two men talked for a short period. Jenny continued to shell the peas. Finally the traveler left. He said he wanted to get to Winchester as soon as possible.

When he was gone, John walked to the porch and sat on the bench with Jenny. "Do you think it was Durham?" he asked.

"Yes," she replied. "I do, may he rest in peace, but I will shed no tears."

John looked at her and smiled. "I don't think we will ever see those two again."

* * * *

Two weeks later in an Indian Village in present day Ohio

Seven Indians walked into the village. Their time raiding had not gone well. They had started with eleven. Instead of being the hunters, they had been hunted. The British and Colonials were too strong. They had captured a few guns, balls and powder, and one woman. They had killed her when they were pursued. A French man, Francois Geoffrey, watched as they entered the village. An object worn around the neck of the leader caught his eye. He walked up to the Indian and asked about it. The Indian took the leather string with the gold coin on it off and handed it to him. The French man took the necklace and placed it on the handsome woman next to him. Her name was Kathleen and he had bought her from the Shawnee. Her father was an escaped slave who found shelter among the Cherokee. She had been captured during a raid and sold to him, but now he loved this woman who was his wife. "For you, my beauty," he said.

She smiled. He could see she was pleased and thankful. The Indian said he had more of the shiny coins. The Frenchman offered to trade. He had whiskey and rum. The Indian was interested. And so for three bottles of whiskey and two bottles of rum, he got ten gold coins. He asked the Indians where they got the coins. They said from a man and woman they had killed near Great Meadows. Geoffrey noted two scalps on the Indian's belt. One was from a woman with long hair. The other came from a bald man.

That was on Braddock's route to Fort Duquesne. He wondered if this was part of the payroll. Perhaps, yes, perhaps it was. Time would tell. He would have to be patient. Time would tell.

Chapter 27

Spring passed into summer on the little farm at the base of Patterson Creek Ridge. Cows had to be milked. Crops had to be weeded. Water had to be brought up to the cabin every day. It was not an easy life for anyone on the frontier. The summer was hot, but the rainfall was good except for several weeks in July when not a drop fell. John had worried the crops might fail if it remained dry much longer, but daily thunderstorms ended that worry. Soon he worried about it being too wet, but such was the life of a farmer. The cow had calved in the spring. John now had to decide whether to keep the heifer for another milk cow, sell her, or butcher her when the weather turned cold. If hunting was good, he would make a choice between two. If not, they would need the meat.

It was a good harvest that year. The bean, squash, and corn crop were bountiful. Hunting was good and John sold the young cow to another man up the valley. Summer turned into fall. The leaves had turned beautiful colors and fallen. John marveled when they did this. There were so many colors to see, not like the little changing green of Ireland. Fall turned into winter. On numerous days, snow flurries were in the air and there had been one snow of about four inches that had now melted. Often the sky was grey and overcast all day. Throughout it all, Jenny had been there. She had been a great help around the house and helped him in the field and with the harvest. At first, she had been reserved, but each day she seemed more relaxed and comfortable with her life on the homestead.

December started cool. Today was Christmas and it was cold. John rose early, very early, before Jenny. Today was to be a special day. Today he would make her breakfast, not the other way around as she always had done. He added more wood to the fire. It was cool in the cabin and he needed it for warmth and to cook. John quickly and quietly prepared the meal. He cooked some bacon over the fire in a skillet. It smelled so good. John heard Jenny stirring in the loft. The smell of the bacon had woken her up. She looked down at John startled and said "Sir, that's my job!"

She descended the ladder from the loft quickly and began helping John with the food. John looked at Jenny and said, "Jenny, today is Christmas and I wanted to do something special for you."

She looked up from her work and replied, "Thank you, sir, but you need not. It's my job to take care of you."

John could see there was no point to arguing with her so they worked on the meal together. When it was done, they sat at the table across from each other. John said a short prayer over the meal and they ate. When they had finished, together they cleared the table. Jenny got John a cup of coffee from the kettle by the fire and gave it to John. He thanked her and said "Jenny, we need to talk. Take a seat here at the table."

Jenny did as he said. John sat across from her. He sipped at the coffee. She looked at him patiently, but he could tell she was curious as to what he wanted to speak to her about. He began, "As you know today is Christmas. On this day, God gave us his Son born of a virgin to save us from our sins. That was the greatest gift ever given. Today I have a gift for you. I give you your freedom."

He pulled Jenny's indentured servant papers from his pocket and wrote "payd in ful" in bold letters on it. John was barely literate. He showed them to Jenny and then he tore them into pieces. Jenny sat there stunned. John rose, walked to the fire, and threw the pieces in. They burned brightly for a minute and fell to the bottom as ash. John turned to the shocked Jenny. "Jenny," he said, "Say something. You're a free woman."

Jenny was overwhelmed. All she could mutter to him was, "Thank you, Sir."

"There will be no more need for 'sir' Jenny," John said. "You can stay here, or if you want, you can walk out that door now and never look back. You're free!"

Jenny opened her mouth to speak, but John cut her off. "There is one more thing. Jenny, I have loved you since the day I first laid eyes on you."

John got down on one knee, took her hand, and looked into Jenny's eyes. "Jenny will you marry me?" he asked.

She rose to her feet. She looked down at John still holding her hand. "John Phares," she began, "if you had asked me yesterday, I would have felt obligated and said no, but today as a free woman, I can choose."

She stopped for what seemed an eternity to John, then she smiled and said, "And today I say YES, John Phares. I WILL marry you. You will be my man, and I will be your woman."

John rose to his feet and put his arms around the waiting Jenny. They hugged and kissed for what seemed forever. Jenny looked into John's eyes and said, "When can we marry?"

John thought for a moment, "The preacher most likely won't be back till spring."

"John," asked Jenny, "isn't God everywhere?"

"Yes, He is," replied John.

"Then let's say our wedding vows to Him right now," Jenny said.

John liked that idea and said, "Yes, let's do that."

He began, "Almighty and all present God, today we stand before you, man and woman, and want to become one. Dear Lord, today I, John take this woman, Jenny, as my wife. I will love her. I will keep her in sickness and in health. I take her for richer or for poorer. I shall be her man and, she shall be my woman. I do this without reservation. So help me God. Amen."

He looked at Jenny. She began, "Almighty and all-knowing God, today I stand before you a free woman. I take this man, John, to be my husband. I do this with no reservation. I will love him. I will cherish him like a precious jewel. I will obey him. He will be my man and I will be his woman from this day until the day I die. Amen."

John and Jenny hugged and kissed. John took Jenny outside. The sun that day was shining bright on the little cabin. John reached under Jenny and picked her up. She let out a surprised gasp. John then carried a laughing Jenny over the threshold into the log cabin. She placed her head on his shoulder and smiled. She had been given a gift beyond her wildest dreams. The rest of the day seemed like a dream to the both of them. That night, Jenny did not sleep in the loft, but downstairs with her new husband. Three months later when the weather turned to spring, Pastor Haskell was able to get to the little community, no longer called Frankfort, but Fort Ashby after the new fort and its commander. At that time he made it official for John and a now pregnant Jenny. Six months later a girl they named Jasmine was born. She would be the first of eight children, six that would live to adulthood. John and Jenny would have many up and downs, many sorrows and joys, in their long lives at the cabin. The community would grow and change, but that's another story.

Chapter 28

Near present day Point Pleasant, WV, at the confluence of the Great Kanawha and the Ohio River

The water lapped lazily at the sides of the two canoes. Paddles dipped rhythmically into the murky waters of the Ohio River. Great blue herons and other kinds of fishing birds stepped stealthily along the riverbanks. The men in the canoes spoke little, each absorbed in his own thoughts. Colonel George Washington, the leader of this expedition, was the most quiet. He reviewed the events of the trip in his mind, especially the unexpected meeting that occurred today on the banks of the Beautiful River, the Ohio, at the point where the Great Kanawha joined it. Colonel Washington left his home and family at Mount Vernon some weeks before. He wanted to see the lands he had finally been granted for his services in the French and Indian War. It had been long in coming. He purchased the rights to additional lands given to other veterans, who got tired of waiting for the King to fulfill his promises. The Colonel wanted to see as much of the land as possible while on the frontier. The road west from Winchester had been filled with settlers. Wagons pulled by horse, or mules, or long horned cattle moved in a steady stream. The wagons were filled and over filled with people and the provisions they would need in their new homes. Occasionally he heard the clucking of chickens coming from the wagons. Some had a milk cow with a bulging udder following along tied to a rope. Sometimes a small calf walked alongside the mother.

He stopped at the Edwards' farm on the Cacapon River. It was good to see Mr. Edwards still in good health in spite of his age. Colonel Washington stopped at several places on Patterson Creek. He visited at the place he remembered Fort Cox had stood, but found nothing at the site. Settlers had taken all the logs from the stockade and built nearby cabins with them. He noted an out of place small sycamore tree growing where he believed the old fort had stood. *What was it doing up on this hill, not by a stream? Sycamores always grow near the water, not up on a hill.*

His thoughts were interrupted by a splash near the boat. A small fish leaped and broke the surface. Perhaps a large fish wanted him for a meal, or maybe the canoe had spooked him. The fish disappeared in the murky liquid and the water was quiet again. He had spent a lot of time in the Patterson Creek valley in his life. Besides Fort Cox, he had stopped at Frankfort, the site of Fort Ashby. Capt. John Ashby, Colonel Washington's old friend, had commanded the fort during the war. The town square was bustling with settlers headed to Fort Cumberland and points west. There were some timbers of the old fort still standing, but most had been carried away like Fort Cox. A cabin likely built of the fort's timbers had been built on the site. He stopped at Lightfoot and Roger McFarland's cabin. Some of the timbers were new. Others were charred black from a past fire. A stout German woman who spoke broken English greeted him. With some difficulty, he discerned that the men he knew had moved somewhere to the west a few years earlier. He was very disappointed. He had wanted to see them and share old memories.

He did stop at John Phares's cabin. John was delighted to see him. His wife, Jenny treated him like family. The Colonel could tell they were very happy together. John was a lucky man to have such a fine wife and five little Phareses running around the crowded cabin.

After leaving the Phares's, the company proceeded down Patterson Creek to the site of Fort Sellers. Again, this fort had suffered the same fate as Fort Cox, but there could be no mistaking its former location near the point where cliffs at the end of the ridge were. Like Fort Cox, it too had a small sycamore tree growing at the remembered location of the old Indian fort. A few shards of timbers still stood where the walls had been. It appeared most of the timbers had been cut off near ground level. This left the outline of the structure discernible, but there was little more. Washington could see it was out with the old and in with the new in the fast-paced world of 1770. They crossed the Potomac River and headed for Fort Cumberland. It was still standing. Indian attacks were still possible, but it lessened everyday as the frontier was pushed westward.

The road to Fort Pitt was full of memories; the camp at Little Meadows, the battle of Fort Necessity at Great Meadows and the glen where Jimonville was killed. Somewhere under the road were the bones of General Edward Braddock. He at last came to the site of the great battle on the Monongehela. The horrors of that terrible day were never far from Colonel Washington's mind. There had been so many times in his life he had escaped death and now he knew why. There had been at least five instances just here in western Pennsylvania. At the river forks they had been met by a company of Indians. An old and respected Delaware Chief, Red Hawk, had called a council fire with the white men. He traveled a long distance to speak with Washington. Though an interpreter he spoke, "I am a chief and ruler of my tribes. I have great influence from the eastern mountains to the waters of the great lakes. I have traveled long to see the young warrior of the great battle. On the day when our guns made the waters and forest run red with the blood of many white soldiers, I first beheld this young chief named Washington. I called to my braves. See the tall and daring warrior. He stands tall on his horse exposed, directing the battle for his troops. Train your guns on him and kill him. He holds his men together. We aimed and fired with guns that fire true and do not know to miss, but all in vain. A power mightier than we protected you. You were under the special shield of the Great Spirit. We stopped firing at you. I fired at you many times. You were an easy target on the horse, but all our shots missed. Now I an old and I speak this word of prophecy. Listen to me! The Great Spirit, the Giver of Life, protects you, Washington and guides your destiny. You will lead a people yet unborn. I pay homage to a man who is a favorite of Heaven, a man who will never die in battle."

These words rang in George Washington's ears even now. He knew that God does direct the paths of a man. *What did the old Chief mean when he said he would "lead a nation yet unborn?" Time would tell. All things happen for a reason and at the ordained time.* For now, he would continue on and check out his lands in the Ohio.

Chapter 29

It had been a warm fall in 1794. John Phares sat on the porch of his cabin at the foot of Patterson Creek Ridge about a mile south of the bustling village of Fort Ashby. The town square was usually filled with homesteaders going west. It was a favorite stopping off point on the main route between Winchester, Virginia, and Cumberland, Maryland. From Cumberland, the settlers would head on to Pittsburgh, Pennsylvania, at the forks of the Ohio. The old stockade fort had been filled with troops earlier this year headed to put down the Whiskey Rebellion in western Pennsylvania. John had gone along. He had been fortunate to have seen and talked to his old friend, George Washington, now President of the United States. If anyone could lead this nation through these troubled times, it was George Washington. George had been happy to see him and stated he was glad to have an old soldier like John at his side. Though John had slowed down, his vision was still good, and he was still able to do a hard day's work.

His wife, Jenny, sat on the porch with him along with several great grandchildren. Their eight children, six that lived, had produced thirty children of their own. They had helped raise some of the grandchildren and now were doing the same with some of the great grandchildren.

All in all, John felt he had a blessed life. A good wife, decent health, lots of children and grandchildren, and a piece of land to call his own. What more could a man ask for?

Then there was the gold. It had provided that little extra when he needed it. He made his first trip back to retrieve all he could carry the spring after General Forbes had chased the French and Indians from Fort Duquesne, now the site of the growing town of Pittsburgh. Over the years he had gone several times and retrieved more of the lost gold. Indian uprisings, civil insurrections, and revolution had cause gaps of years between the trips. On his way home from his recent trip to western Pennsylvania with General Washington, he had stopped at the old site, but been unable to find the last remaining gold in the cannons. Too much had changed. He knew he had been close, but he came up empty this time. He had always told Jenny when he went on these trips he was going "sangin," that is, after ginseng. It still brought a good price in these parts. He knew she knew better, but she never pressed the issue. He had his secrets from the past and she did, too. Some things were just best left alone. *Let sleeping dogs lie*, John could still hear his mother say.

Some of the gold he kept hidden in the fissure cave in the ridge behind his house. He had buried other stashes of gold at the sites of frontier forts in his area. He planted a buttonwood tree to mark the spot. Some of the gold had fallen from his saddle through a tear on one trip. Some had ended up in a rain-swollen river, when his packhorse stumbled in the swift water, drown and was carried away in the current. All in all he had retrieved most of the gold, but he had chosen to use little of it. He knew that newfound wealth attracts attention, most of it unwanted. He was also afraid it would make him lazy or a snob like the English upper class he had met and observed. He would keep it for himself if he ever needed it, or perhaps one of his descendants sometime in the future would put it to a good use. Perhaps, time would tell.

John looked over at his grandson's boy. "Jesse," he said, let's go check on the eggs. Let's see which hens are still layin' and which ones will be dinner."

"That will be fun, Grandpa!" the young boy replied.

The two walked to the hen house. John looked out over the valley in front of the cabin. A mist was forming in the valley he called a hollow. It would be foggy tonight and in the morning. It was beautiful. John knew he had his own little piece of heaven right here. He was a blessed man. Good wife, good family, good land, good friends, and the Good Lord above. No amount of gold could buy treasures like these. He would sleep well tonight.

"Hey, Grandpa! Did you forget we were after eggs?" questioned a young voice.

"Boy, you get them, would you? And be careful not to break any."

"Sure will, Grandpa."

With that, the youth ran into the chicken coop and immediately the hens began to cackle as he searched for the eggs. John walked to a large old stump and sat down on it. Yes, he was a blessed man. When the Good Lord called him home to Heaven, he would die a happy man. But he was in no hurry for that. There was still so much to see and do here before he took his eternal sleep. He smiled to himself.

"Hey, Grandpa. Could you help me with all these eggs?"

John turned toward the young voice. Jesse had his arms full of eggs. "Sure can. I'm coming as fast as I can." Yes, he was a very blessed man.

Chapter 30

The bone-chilling sleet continued to pelt the window of the farmhouse on that early January morn in 1862. General Stonewall Jackson of the Confederate Army sat at the table. He was using the house near the Indian Mound Cemetery at Romney as his headquarters. After the march from Winchester, Virginia, his frozen southern troops, not used to this kind of weather, had balked at continuing on to Jackson's final objective, the vital town of Cumberland, Maryland. The B & O Railroad that supplied the Union cause must be severed.

An open-hearth fireplace took the chill from the room. He laid his spectacles down by his well-worn Bible. Federal troops controlled western Virginia and there was talk of Lincoln making that area a new state loyal to the Union. If he had anything to do about it, there would be only one Virginia, not two. He had been born in Clarksburg, Virginia in western Virginia. His troops were firmly in control of Romney for now, but for how long? This region had exchanged hands many times already in this civil war. How long would they hold on this time?

His eyes dropped to the coins on the table before him. Ten gold coins. Ten old gold coins. Ten old gold British coins. Could this really be part of General Braddock's gold that was lost north of his present position, somewhere in Pennsylvania? The Yankee prisoner they had seemed to think so. He said he found the coins in a river there. The troops that interrogated him threatened him with death if he did not tell all he knew, but that was all he knew. General Jackson did not approve of his soldiers' tactics, but now he had the information just the same.

If Braddock's gold payroll could be found, the Confederacy could use it to repay the French for the gold they had given the new Southern government.

General Jackson would love to strike at the Yankees north in Maryland and Pennsylvania, but he was tied down here. He would pass this valuable information on to General Robert E. Lee. He knew Lee wanted to take the fight to the Yankees there soon. Perhaps this would influence his decision as to when and where. Perhaps, but for now he would go back to his Bible and read more of David, the warrior King of ancient Israel. War could and would wear down the soul. The General needed to be refreshed. He opened his book to the Psalms. "The Lord is my shepherd; I shall not want. He makes me to lie down in green pastures; He leads me beside the still waters. He restores my soul; He leads me in the path of righteousness for His name's sake. Yea, though I walk through the valley of the shadow of death, I will fear no evil; for Thou are with me; Thy rod and Thy staff they comfort me."

The General smiled to himself. If David with all his troubles could do it, he could, too. "The Lord is my shepherd," he whispered to himself. "Yea, though I walk through the valley of the shadow of death, I will fear no evil: for thou art with me; thy rod and thy staff they comfort me."

Chapter 31

Spring 1994

Michael Levy sat at the porch of the old house near Patterson Creek watching the sunrise. He loved this time of day. It gave him a time to think. Three months ago he got the bad news from his doctor, chronic heart deterioration. He had six months to two years to live. His heart would continue to weaken. There was no cure. One day it would just give out and he would be gone. He should not exert himself strenuously. There should be no heavy lifting. He had called his boss, the Voice, and let him know this would be his last crop for him and why. The Voice expressed his thanks for many years of service and asked if there was anything he could do for him. Michael said no. He had plenty of money for end of life decisions and was setting his affairs in order. The Voice again made sure Michael knew if there was anything he could do to just ask for it.

Michael was bored. The marijuana crop in the trailers that served as grow houses had been harvested and he had his share of the profits from the Voice. And it had been very good and very profitable. He was bored, very bored. He had been searching for the phantom Braddock's Gold for years and that was at a dead end. Michael had accumulated his own small library at the old farmhouse. Most of the books were related in one way or the other to his search for the illusive treasure. And he had a goodly number of books by Tony Hillerman and Louis

L'Amour. Michael loved reading about the American West.

And now he was bored. Michael needed some tires for his old car. The present tires were thin and would never get him thought the winter. Money was no object. He had plenty. The old tires on snowy roads could kill him before his heart finally gave out and he was in no hurry to go. He saw a tire ad in the paper from Walmart and it was a decent price for American-made tires. He drove to the store, picked out the tires he wanted, and waited in the 'guest lobby' as they called the waiting room at the store. Michael bought a Coke from the machine and sat down. His eyes spotted a large ad posted on the wall. It said, "Bored? Need money? Walmart has a job for you." Michael had nothing else to do, so he walked over to the store human resources and applied. To his surprise they hired him as a greeter and wanted him to start as soon as possible. They agreed on next Monday. When he got back to the auto section, the service man was waiting. The new tires were on his car, the paperwork was done, and he could go. What a surprise this day had been. He went for tires, got them and got hired. As he drove back to the old house, he became aware of a growling stomach.

Michael stopped at Linda's Old Furnace Restaurant. He ordered a hearty breakfast, two scrambled eggs, home fries, grits, and two strips of bacon. Michael was Jewish, though his family had been secular for years. And he loved the taste of bacon. A cup of coffee rounded out the delicious meal. He left a big tip for the waitress and paid his bill. As he walked to the door, he noted the many pictures on the walls, mainly pictures of Indians. *The owner must surely love Indians,* he thought. The rest of the trip down the crooked Old Furnace Road and to the old house he called home was uneventful.

Monday morning found Michael at Walmart. He filled out the required employment papers, watched the required company information videos and one hour later was greeting shoppers at the front door. And he liked it.

At break time, a woman came up and relieved him. "You need to be back in fifteen minutes," she said and he was off to the break room.

"Well hello, you must be Michael, the new greeter," said a smiling woman in her late forties. Then she gave him a big hug. "God loves you and so do I."

To say the least Michael was pleasantly surprised. It had been a long time since the old bachelor had felt the milk of genuine human kindness. The woman continued, "I'm Mary, Mary Miltenberger. I'm glad to meet you."

Mary was friendly to everyone and always ready to tell you about Jesus. Michael found her a little pushy at first, but there was no denying the love she had for others. He could see it in her eyes. You can't fake that and he soon grew used to Mary just as she was. From then on, Michael looked forward to seeing her at break time. And sometimes she'd bring brownies. He had never tasted brownies like she made. They were beyond delicious.

Two months later found Michael still enjoying his job at Walmart, but he could feel the strength leaving his body. Mary had given him two books to read, a *Living Bible* and *The Case for Christ* by Lee Stroebel. He thanked her and spent his free time reading them. He knew he was dying. He could feel it. He wondered how many other people never came to grips with dying. They just go on in denial they would ever die and then do just that. Mary told him all about how Jesus' death on the cross paid the price to ransom us from our sins and death. And one day as he sat on the porch of the old house, he made his peace with Jesus. He could hardly wait to tell Mary the good news. When he saw her at work, he told her all. She said, "I knew it. There was something different about you. I saw life in your eyes."

And then she welcomed him into God's fellowship with a big hug as only Mary could give. Others in the store commented on Michael spirit even as they could see him getting weaker.

Two weeks later, Michael went to Fort Ashby's only attorney and drew up a will and last wishes. He wanted his body to be cremated and his ashes scattered in Israel. His nephew Mike was to get the farm after he had completed this last request of his Uncle and only then. The attorney would take care of all cremation arrangement and get necessary papers for transporting the remains on the airlines and through Customs here and in Israel.

One week after that, Michael notified the local bank he needed to withdraw fifty thousand dollars from his account. They had the money ready for him at the designated time. Shortly afterward, the Catholic Church in Fort Ashby where Mary Miltenberger worshiped and the synagogue in Cumberland received a package containing fifty one hundred dollar bills. Another 40 churches of various denominations reported getting mail containing ten one hundred dollar bills each. The local paper picked up the story of the generous anonymous donor and spread the good news. Michael smiled when he read the story. His hope was that his ill-gotten wealth could do some good. Six days later while at work, Michael felt pain, a bad pain in his chest. He sat on the bench near the door. Mary was working the floor that day. She saw his distress and went to him. "Michael, are you all right?" she asked.

He looked into those eyes of love, the eyes of an angel he believed. "Yes Mary, because of you I am." And then he died in the comforting arms of Mary. He had gone to meet his Savior.

Another lost sheep had been brought back home by a woman working her mission field.

Chapter 32

You could have knocked Mike over with a feather when he got the call from the lawyer in Fort Ashby telling him he was the benefactor of his Uncle Michael's will. They had never been close. He had only seen his uncle a few times in his adult life, but then there really wasn't much family left. Most of them had died in the Holocaust in Europe during World War II. The lawyer asked him to come to his office to sign some necessary papers. Mike was shown the will of his uncle. He got all of Uncle Michael's worldly possessions after he took his remains on their last journey. Uncle Michael wanted his cremated remains scattered in Israel. Mike agreed readily. The lawyer purchased airline tickets and filled out the final paperwork the various federal agencies required for transporting human remains. A week later Mike found himself sitting in a Continental Airlines 767 bound from Newark, New Jersey to Ben Gurion Airport in Tel Aviv, Israel. He looked at the other passengers on the plane. Some were obvious Christian tourists going to the Holy Land. Others were Hasidic Jews of various flavors. They had beards of different sizes. Some had side curls. The men all had head coverings. Some had kippas that looked like beanies. The others had hats of different styles. Several reminded him of Indiana Jones's fedoras. Sitting next to him was a clean-cut man of about thirty. Mike noted him also looking over the four hundred plus passengers on the plane. He noticed Mike doing the same. "Hi, my name's Sam. What's yours?" the clean-cut man asked.

"Mike, Mike Levy," he replied. "What are you goin' be doing in Israel?"

"I'm in the reserves," he answered. "My outfit will be practicing maneuvers with the IDF, that's the Israeli Defense Forces. And you?"

Mike said, "Thank you very much for your service to our county. What am I doing in Israel? My uncle died and he wanted his ashes spread in the Holy Land."

Sam said he was sorry to hear of his uncle's passing. How long would he be in Israel? Where was he staying while there? Mike said he did not know where he was staying, but he would be coming back after two full days there. Sam said he had been in Israel before. He could catch public transportation, Egged Bus Lines, at the airport and go to a place that rented rooms just outside of Jerusalem. The buses passed by regularly for easy connection anywhere in the country. And the rooms were reasonable and clean. Mike thanked him for all the information. They chatted for a while longer. The movie came on the screen and they began to watch it.

It wasn't that good and Mike soon fell asleep. Hours later he awoke. From the movement of the airplane, he could tell they were descending. Sam next to him spoke, "Man, you were sleeping like the dead. It won't be long till we are at the airport."

So it was. Soon they landed and were in a line for processing by Israeli Customs.

It was now Mike's turn. "Passport," the Customs man said in English. "How long will you be staying and what will you be doing here?"

"I will be here today and tomorrow and leaving the following day for home." Mike handed him the necessary papers for carrying his uncle's remains. "And I will be scattering my uncle's ashes here in the Holy Land. It was his last request."

The young man frowned. "It would be best if you did not do this in a cemetery. The Orthodox could cause trouble for you. It's not their way. And they can be nasty when they don't get their way. What transport do you have while here?"

Mike told him of his plans to use the public bus transport while here. The young officer thought for a minute and said, "I know of place just outside of the town around Jerusalem that you could scattered the remains. It's near a bus stop with regular service every half hour. It is on the side of a hill overlooking the Judean Wilderness and the Dead Sea. The hills are covered with grass that is a golden brown."

"That sounds like parts of California," said Mike.

"Yes, it is very similar," the young man said. "That is where I grew up, before I made aliyah. When I get home sick, I go out there. It is peaceful. Your uncle would like it I believe."

The young soldier gave Mike instructions on how to get there from where he was staying and soon Mike was on an Egged bus heading for Jerusalem. He gave the driver, who spoke some English, a five dollar bill, told him where he wanted to get off and got change in Israeli coins. After several stops along the highway, the bus stopped again and the driver yelled and motioned to Mike this was his departure point. He got off with his burdens and walked about one hundred feet to the building that Sam had described. Yes, the owner said they had rooms. They were as Sam had described. Mike put his things in the clean but utilitarian room. *Kinds of like an Israeli version of Motel 6. Spend a night, not a fortune*, he thought.

He studied the brochure he got on the bus for the schedules and routes. He had plenty of time today to get there by bus to the place overlooking the Judean Wilderness the Customs man told him about. Mike left the building, walked to a small sidewalk vender selling falafels. There was no line at the kiosk on the busy street. He got one and bit in. It was nothing to write home about. He choked it down and ran to the bus stop to catch a bus that had just arrived. Mike carried a large bottle of water and the box containing his uncle's ashes in his pack hanging from his shoulder. Soon he was changing buses at the Central Bus Station in Jerusalem. It wasn't but a half hour drive to the place in the Judean Wilderness. He got off the bus and looked around. It was as peaceful and starkly beautiful as had been described. *Uncle Michael would like this place* he thought. Mike stood quietly and looked off to the east toward the hills in Jordan on the other side of the Jordan River. The wind moved the short grass on the eroded, rocky hill slopes in waves. Mike basked in the harsh desert beauty for about five minutes. After that, he reached into the backpack, removed the box containing the ashes, took the lid off, paused slightly, and threw the ashes with the wind. He stood there motionless for what seemed a long minute. *Yes, Uncle Michael would have liked this.* Mike sat down on the bench facing the wilderness at the bus stop and enjoyed the solitude broken only occasionally by a vehicle that soon disappeared over the hills. A bus came ten minutes later and Mike got on. One hour and a half later, Mike was turning the key to his room. He took a quick shower and went to bed. It had been a full day. He had done what he had come for. Tomorrow he would do some sightseeing. *What could he learn of what being Jewish meant?* But now he was tired, very tired. Jet lag had set in. He went to the small bathroom, brushed his teeth, and used the funky water-saving toilet. After that he turned to the small sink, poured some water, and drank it down. His eyes caught his reflection in the mirror. *Lucky dog*, he thought. *You're gonna have your own place when you get back to the USA.* He smiled slightly, turned, and walked to the single bed in the corner of the spartan room. Slowly, he sat down on the bed, and rolled over on his side. He could hear the traffic on the street just outside old building. In a very short time, he was sound asleep, snoring, and dreaming dreams he would never remember in the morning.

Chapter 33

Mike rose late that morning. The jet lag seemed to be gone, but he knew the trip back would give him another case of it. He dressed quickly and headed out the door. There were no restaurants nearby, only the falafel booth guy and he did not seem to be busy though there were lots of people on the sidewalks. Mike could see an Egged bus coming in the distance, so he ran to the stop. He would find something to eat later. Besides, the little food booth hadn't been very satisfactory. The food gave him heartburn.

Shortly he was at the Central Bus Station. He had to run if he wanted to catch the bus he was looking for, the one they called "The Time Elevator." It was getting ready to leave. Line 99 was advertised as a '3000 year journey through the history of Jerusalem,' and he did not want to miss it. Passengers could get off and then back on at any of twenty-five historical sites on the route in the city without limit. Mike had only this day in Jerusalem and he wanted to use it wisely. Much of his valuable time had already passed. The bus went by many ancient buildings and some modern ones, but all made with the same stone, Jerusalem stone. He caught his first glimpse of the old city wall near the New Gate. The bus continued on its route, stopping regularly at various sites, several of them being modern high rise hotels. It rounded many turns in this ancient city built on steep hills and valleys. On the Jericho Road, the bus stopped near the Lion's Gate and Mike got off.

The bus pulled back into traffic and Mike stood on a busy sidewalk bustling with tourists and towns' people. To his left was the Kidron Valley and behind that the Mount of Olives, now covered in Jewish tombs. He saw several beautiful churches, one Greek Orthodox and another with the sign that read "Church of All Nations." To the south was the walled up Eastern Gate, also known as the Golden Gate where the Messiah would enter the city at the chosen time.

At this time Mike's stomach reminded him of its emptiness. It growled loudly. Mike thought it would start eating his backbone if he didn't feed it soon. He walked up the steep street to the Lion's Gate, build by Suliman the Magnificent. Two young Israeli soldiers dressed in drab green and carrying M16s stood to the side below the Lion carved in the old wall. They about ten feet apart and their alert eyes scanned the crowds of people looking for any signs of trouble. Mike approached the closer one cautiously and asked "Son, could you tell me where I could get a good meal around here?"

The guard looked at him suspiciously. Mike smiled at the gun-toting soldier. He motioned with his finger for Mike to follow him. They walked the short distance to the other soldier and the first said something to him in Hebrew. The second young soldier looked at Mike and said, "Sir, can I help you? My friend speaks only Hebrew and Czech and did not understand you."

"Yes," Mike said somewhat relieved, "I'm looking for a place to get a bite to eat quickly. I missed my breakfast and I'm getting hungry."

The second young soldier thought for a minute and said, "Stay on this road, it's the Via Dolorosa. About one block up the street, on the left, is a small kiosk eatery run by an old Muslim man, called Alean. It's got the best *shawarmas* in Israel. I stop there regularly."

Mike asked, "What's a *shawarma*? I've never heard of that."

"You may know it as a gyro," the young man said.

"Oh, yah, I know what that is," Mike said. "Thanks, say are you an American? You sound like you come from the Midwest."

"You are correct, Texas, my name's Jonathan," he answered. "And your name is?"

"My name's Mike, Mike Levy."

Jonathan responded "Mike Levy, you're Jewish. Are you here to make aliyah?"

"What's this aliyah?" Mike asked.

"Aliyah means 'to ascend.' It's the term used when Jews return from the Diaspora, the dispersion. All Jews have the right of return and become citizens of Israel," Jonathan said.

"I didn't know that," said Mike. "Actually I'm here to finish some personal business for my uncle."

After this Mike and the young man chatted about the USA. Jonathan said he was a Texas Ranger fan and Mike said he rooted for the Baltimore Orioles, even though they hadn't won a World Series since 1983. Mike thanked the soldiers for their help and he was off on the Via Dolorosa. He found Alean's shortly and there was a long line. Mike hoped the wait would be worth it. It was. The soldier was right. The food here was great. Mike made a mental note to only stop at street food venders with lines of customers willing to wait.

He stopped at St. Anna's Church and listened to a group of tourists sing in Portuguese in an ancient doomed room. The acoustics were perfect and the singing was beautiful even though Mike didn't understand a word. He walked further down the street and found himself in a *souk*, an Arab Market. The street was narrow and the merchant's goods for sale in front of their small shops made the street even smaller. Fearing pickpockets, Mike took his wallet from the back pocket and put it in his front pocket. He marveled at the various goods. Everything was for sale: souvenirs, spices, cloths, coffee, food, and luggage. One place looked like a drugstore somewhat. There was even an open air butcher shop with the skinned carcasses of sheep and goats hanging with their blood dripping into the street. This went on for two blocks and soon Mike was at the entrance to the Wailing Wall, also known as the Western Wall. Mike went in the security booth that all persons must go through before being admitted. He took off his watch, belt, and emptied his pockets. Then he removed his shoes that had metal shanks. He went in the metal monitor and it beeped. Mike was surprised. What had he forgotten? The young soldier in drab green at the monitor looked at Mike and said, "Sir, remove your hat."

Mike handed him his hat. The soldier took it, looked inside, and felt around the inside. He found nothing. Then he felt the brim and noticed the wire running on the outside brim. He laid the hat on the belt and ran it through the x-ray machine. "Now go through," the soldier said.

Mike did and there was no alarm this time. He collected his things from the belt and put himself back together. He walked out of the building and saw the wall and all the people involved in various religious ceremonies. The men were on the left and the women on the right, separated by a wall about 4 ½ feet tall. Jews of all flavors, Christians, and tourist prayed at the Wall. Mike's hard heart was moved. He walked to the wall and prayed, "Lord, I feel your presence here and you know the kind of a man I am. You know I'll never change, but please have mercy on this sinner." And then he wept, something he hadn't done since he was a child.

Slowly Mike turned from the wall, wiped the tears from his checks and walked away. He had much to do before the day was over. He noted the Al-Aqsa Mosque and the imposing Dome of the Rock, high above him on the Temple Mount. He was now back on the street. He exited the Old City by the Dung Gate. Mike walked the short distance to the City of David, the heart of ancient Jerusalem, the city of the Kings and the prophets. He looked at the exhibits, some of them three millennium old. Beneath his feet Hezekiah's men dug the tunnel 1,500 feet through solid rock using hand picks and torches for light to bring water to the ancient city on the defensible hill.

Mike left the Israeli National Park and soon was back on the Line 99 bus. It took a twisting course past many stops. As it passed the Zion Gate, he saw the many bullet holes in the ancient walls where the Israeli troops fought their way into the Old City during the Six Day was in 1969. Mike was running late so he skipped stop twenty, the Herzl Museum, Herzl was the father of modern Hebrew. But what Mike really wanted to see was Yad Vashem, the Holocaust Memorial. Almost all his family had died or disappeared during this terrible time. Mike's mother had talked little about this. It was just too painful for her. What he did know was that his mother and uncle got out on forged papers. There was only enough money for papers for two people and all the rest had been left behind and vanished during the war. Uncle Michael was much younger than his sister and was passed off as her son during the escape to Switzerland. There Mike's mother discovered she was pregnant with Mike. Would there be some trace of the Levys in the memorial? He hoped for an answer, but expected none.

Chapter 34

The red bus rounded another bend and yet another and pulled up to the forty-five acre site known as Yad Vashem. Mike walked through the entrance gate and saw the sign that announced, "And to them I give in my house and within my walls a memorial and a name, a 'yad vashem', that shall not be cut off. Isaiah 56:5."

He began the short but introspective walk to the visitor center. There he got an informative brochure on the complex and grabbed a quick meal at the cafeteria. He asked for a cheeseburger, but was told the eatery was kosher and all he could get was a plain hamburger. He got that and was served sliced vegetables, mainly peppers, tomatoes, and carrots, instead of French fries as he expected, but then, he wasn't back in the USA. He purchased a large coffee to drink, asked for milk to add to it, but was told it was not kosher, so they gave him some non-dairy creamer. This kosher thing obviously made sense to the locals, but it just puzzled Mike. *Oh well*, he thought, *when in Rome, or Israel, do as the Romans, I mean Israelis do*. Tomorrow he would be heading for home. There things would be back to normal, cheeseburgers and milk in his coffee.

He walked down the tree-lined walkway called the Avenue of the Righteous Among the Nations that led to the Holocaust History Museum. Stopping at a large plaque, he began to read the story about one of the Gentile Righteous. "I believe that it was really due to Loren that I am alive today and not so much for his material aid, as for his constantly reminding me by his presence, there still existed a just world outside our own, something and someone still pure and whole for which it was worth surviving." Peter Levi.

Mike just stared at the plaque, Peter Levi. His father's name was Peter. The last name was spelled differently, but could it be? There were probably many men with that name. His mother had told him once a friendly clergyman had faked baptism certificates. With these his mother and uncle were able to obtain forged papers at a high cost and been able to escape the Nazis by way of Switzerland.

He entered the nearly five hundred foot long building known as the Holocaust History Museum. There the story of Shoah, the Holocaust, or Hell was told from the view of the Jews who lived and died under the Nazis and their collaborators. He passed the many artifacts, testimonials, photos, documents, multimedia, and videos. The stories of struggle, death, and survival touched the hard heart of Mike. He walked to the very end to the Hall of Names. In the center was a suspended large cone, maybe twenty feet across at the bottom. The inside was lined from bottom to top with pictures of victims of the Shoah. Around him rose symbolic tombstones from the floor filled out by survivors in memory of their loved ones.

He left the building and walked the short distance to the Hall of Remembrance, a square, gray basalt structure built to pay respect to the martyred dead. The names of the 22 Nazi murder sites were carved in the floor. A memorial flame next to a crypt of cremated remains, ashes from the concentration camps, burned. He was weary from all the death, still he knew he would go on.

Mike walked past the spire called the Pillar of Heroism that commemorated the Jewish Resistance. He stopped at the Children's Memorial. It was for the one and a half million children who had died. *So much killing,* thought Mike. *And why had they not spared even the children?*

He continued onto the Memorial of the Deportees. It was a monument to the millions of Jews transported from all over Europe by cattle cars to the extermination camps. The railroad car sat at the end of an incomplete bridge segment. *Anyone in the car would plunge into annihilation and oblivion,* he thought. *Or did it symbolize hope as it faced the hills of Jerusalem and Israel? Probably both.* Mike then saw the Warsaw Ghetto Square story presented. Here the Jews fought the Nazis bravely with anything they had before they died. Next, he walked back to the monument to the French town of Le Chambon-sur-Lignon. The Protestant town that suffered so much persecution from Catholic France had provided a haven and sheltered the Jews.

Lastly, he stopped at the place that had nagged him since he had first walked in the complex. He had to know about his family. *Were there any records of what happened to them? What of this Peter Levi?* Mike found a middle-aged woman to help him. He gave her the information she needed. Soon she returned with papers and pictures. Mike looked through them carefully. He turned a page and with a start, saw a man's face in a picture that looked like his own. It read "Peter Levi." The information under it said he had survived the Nazis and escaped to Italy. The rest of his known family died in the war. He walked all the way to Palestine, modern day Israel, and died in the War for Independence. A great load came off Mike's heart. He had found his father. He had found his family. He had found his roots.

The article continued. It said that Peter Levi was buried at Mount Hertzl. *Mount Hertzl, why he had just passed that place earlier on the bus.* He had to go there. He had to see for himself. The bus ride back seemed more like a dream than reality to the stunned Mike Levy. The bus dropped him and other passengers off at the site. As a mass, they walked into the small building at the graveyard and were directed into a dark room with a movie screen on one wall. All remained quiet. After about a minute, a video started. It told the story of the vision of Theodor Hertzl, an early Zionist who helped start the nation of Israel. It was through his efforts the dead Hebrew language had been reborn. The film continued on as it told the story of the Jews and Israel for nearly an hour. As it was ending, it gave instructions to those present on how to find friends and relatives buried at the site. The film ended and the room went dark for what seemed an eternity though it was only ten to fifteen seconds. A light came on as the exit doors opened. There was very little noise as the crowd left the room. Those who did speak did so in hushed tones. Mike walked out and went to one of the counters where an elderly woman sat. "May I help you?" the old woman asked.

Mike looked at the wrinkled, smiling face and noted the crude numbered tattoo on her arm. "Yes," he said. "I think my father, Peter Levi, is buried here. Can you help me find where?"

She nodded her head and began leafing through a large, well-worn book. It did not take long for her to find an answer and give him directions to the grave. He thanked her, turned, and began his walk to the site. He was eager to get there, but it seemed he was walking through a long tunnel even though he was outside with trees around him. He rounded a bend in the walkway and in front of him, just as the old woman at the desk had said, was the gravesite. It was about 12 feet square and raise 2 feet above the surrounding walkway. Each side had four flat gravestones. He looked at a stone. There was writing in Hebrew that he could not read, but also in English which he could. "Eli Klein" it said, "Killed in the Battle for Jerusalem." He looked at another stone and another. On the fourth stone, he saw the name, "Peter Levi," and the inscription, "Killed in the Battle at Kibbutz Yad Mordechai." Tears rolled from his eyes. He had found his father. An attendant for the cemetery was nearby and saw his distress. He came to Mike and asked something in Hebrew. "What?" Mike chocked out.

"Are you okay, sir?"

"Yes, I found my father." Mike pointed to the stone.

The young man was silent for a full minute as Mike wept. He cleared his throat and said, "It is good you found him. Now you can have closure."

Mike wiped the tears from his face and nodded yes.

"And others have found him, too," the young man added.

"How do you know that?" the surprised Mike asked.

"See the small stones on the grave stone? Here in Israel, we don't leave flowers when we visit the dead. We leave a stone."

Mike looked at the stones on the grave. Seven and one was brightly painted crudely like done by a small child. Somewhere in Israel he had family. Somewhere.

The rest of Mike's time in Israel seemed like a dream. Somewhere nearby was family that did not know he even existed. He would like to find them, but he had no time. That would have to wait until a later time.

Chapter 35

Spring 1995
Old farmhouse near the town of Patterson Creek

There was much work to do at the old farm. Uncle Michael had left the old grow house operation in moth balls so to speak. The old windmills and solar panels needed attention. The gas generators had to be worked on. The industrial grade batteries for storing electric for the operation were dead and needed a deep charge. Freezing temperatures had broken some of the water lines in the trailers. On and on it went. Mike showed Alan how to perform the necessary work. Daily he would leave in the truck, which now had high plywood sides in the bed and a tarp to cover the contents. When be returned, the truck was full of supplies for the grow house. One day it was boxes of Jiffy 7's, plastic pots of varying sizes, and fertilizer. Several days he returned with the truck loaded with growing medium; peat moss, vermiculite, and potting soil. Mike instructed Alan how to start the plants from the high quality seeds.

First hydrate the Jiffy 7's. When they had expanded fully, take a pencil and make a hole about one inch deep in the peat of the Jiffy 7's. Next, plant two seeds in each of them. Keep them moist and warm. In a few days, the seedlings would come up. If two came up, pick the most vigorous one to keep and eliminate the other. Alan was very busy. Mike told him it would be a lot of work at first but once the crop was up and growing, it would be a lot easier. As it was still cool outside they kept all the small plants in one walled off end of the trailer. This was well heated and kept lighted eighteen hours a day. Watering at this time was done with a watering can. The fluid contained the maximum amount of liquid fertilizer for optimum growth of the tender plants. Soon they would be transferred to 4-inch pots and the men would start eliminating the male plants that did not produce the desirable and potent buds that could make seeds.

The plants grew quickly with the attentive care. Still the men made a point of keeping every Saturday as a downtime for rest. Friday night Mike would leave the old farm on the hill and return late the following day. He never said where he went, but he always had fresh groceries from Martin's in Cumberland. One week Alan asked Mike to get some scrapple, also known as pon haus, for him. His mother had made it often for him and he missed her and her cooking. Mike had never heard of it, but found it at the store and got some for Alan. That following Sunday morning Alan fried some up in a pan on the stove. Mike tried a small amount, but really didn't care for it, so Alan ate both servings covered in syrup. "You don't know what you are missin'," he told Mike.

Mike replied, "To each his own."

The following week Mike brought back some gefilte fish for Alan to try.

He nearly blew his dinner as the slimy, gelatinous fish blob went down his throat. Alan questions him, "What are you trying to do, poison me?"

To which Mike replied, "To each his own," as he happily downed his treat.

It was on evenings when Alan still had a little energy left and on the days off that Alan explored the house and farm. Mike told him to make himself at home. Alan asked if he could look at the extensive library Mike's uncle had left. Mike, who was not much of a book person, told him to knock himself out. "Read all you want. There's not much to do here. Maybe you can find something interesting."

Aside from the daily paper that continued to appear and the radio, there really wasn't much to do after work was done.

The first month was very busy. There was so much to do to just to get the old place and the grow house back functioning properly. The old drip irrigation watering system gave them fits. Everything was clogged. They got that all cleaned out, but then the fertilizer injection system wouldn't work. Finally after much trial and error, they got it working. Alan found an old West Virginia Highways map and was able to figure out exactly where the old farm was on the map. He studied the roads and details. He knew this could come in helpful someday.

Uncle Michael had quite a collection of books. Alan concluded he must have been a history buff, especially local history. There were many books on early American history. Some were Colonial. Some were on the Civil War, but most were on the French and Indian War. There was also a moderately used cheap-made Bible and several other books with religious themes. Alan had always liked history in school. Many events in American history happened not far from his home in Hagerstown. Several important battles of the French and Indian War had been fought just northwest of there, near Pittsburgh. Gettysburg and bloody Antietam were just a stone's throw away. George Washington traveled through the area many times and led his rebellious colonial troops against the British Redcoats along the eastern coast. And the National anthem was written on a ship in Baltimore harbor during the War of 1812, again against the bloody British. He could remember school field trips to Fort McKinley in Baltimore, Harpers Ferry, and Fort Frederick, near Hancock, Maryland. He would look at the books some more later, but now he was tired and needed sleep. They would be there tomorrow.

The next four days, Mike left early every morning and returned late in the afternoon with the truck loaded with more bags of peat moss, vermiculite, and high grade potting soil. Alan spent the days mixing the three equally and filling the many pots by hand. It was hard work. Soon the growing plants would need transplanted to the larger pots. Alan filled the last of them Friday afternoon.

As usual, Mike made to leave. "I'll be back late tomorrow. Keep an eye on the old place and the operation. We don't want to disappoint the Voice. Anything you want special from the store?"

"Yah," Alan said. "How about getting some Chinese carry-out, chips, and a six pack of Coke?"

"Consider it done," Mike replied. "Did you find anything interesting in my uncle's library?"

"Lots of history books, but I like history," Alan said. "We've been so busy. I hadn't got any reading done. I hope to do some while you are gone."

"Well enjoy the free time, but take a look at the old tractor and side bar mower. See if it will fire up and work. We will need it to cut the field. And while you are looking around here, keep an eye out for a rifle. I think my uncle had one. I think he has it hidden somewhere around here." Alan said he would and Mike was soon off down the farm lane toward the main road.

He fixed himself a TV dinner, washed it down with Gatorade, and had a Fiji apple for dessert. "An old gun around here," Alan thought aloud. "There could be a varmint or two around here that needs shooting. You never know."

Alan walked out to the cliffs on the west side behind the house. Spring was beautiful up on the hill. He could see the town of Patterson Creek through the trees and the stream the town was named for. The town was located where the smaller stream joined the larger Potomac. The low rumble of a distant train reached his ear. It would soon pass on the tracks far below. It had been a dry spring so far. The waterways were low and clear. Near the junction of the two streams, Alan could see that the larger one was only, he guessed, about a foot deep and one hundred feet wide. He wondered if in olden days people had forded the river there. The answer to that question would have to wait. The sun was going down, He was tired and soon he was in bed sleeping soundly.

The next morning after breakfast, he checked on the grow house. It was okay. He went to the shed where the old green and yellow John Deere tractor sat. Alan checked the gas. It was full and then he checked the oil. It was half a quart low and dirty. It needed changing. He would tell Mike and he would get what they needed. A new oil filter would be wise too.

Alan dusted off the seat. The key was in the ignition. He tried it. To his surprise, the tractor coughed twice and started up. *Will wonders never cease?* he thought. That was something his mother had often said. He backed the tractor out of the shed and drove to the field in front of the house. He fiddled with the controls and the cutter bar lowered to the ground. He pulled another lever and the cutter blade moved back and forth rapidly. To see if he could master it, he drove out to the old sycamore tree and began to cut around it. He cut close to an acre of the grass that was a foot tall. Alan would cut the rest later when it really needed it. He drove the tractor back to the barn and parked it inside. *That was easy,* he thought. *About time I got a break.*

A shiny something sticking out from under a dusty tarp, caught his eye. He pulled the tarp from the hidden object. He had found a bicycle and it looked to be in pretty good shape, fat soft tires and all. Alas searched around and located a hand air pump. He pumped up the tires and half expected them to go flat, but the air held, for now. He would check later to see if they remained full. *This old farm had a lot of surprises. I wonder what else I can find?*

Chapter 36

Later in the day Alan checked on the bike tires and sure enough, they continued to hold air. He took the bike out of the shed and rode it down the farm lane to the state secondary road and back to the farmhouse. It was in pretty good shape for the shape it was in. From then on, he used it to get the paper that continued to show up in the box next to the gate at the end of the farm lane.

When Mike got back that evening, he showed him the tractor and the bike. Mike was impressed. "Very good," he said, "I can see you've been busy. No grass is gonna grow under your feet. You are always moving."

They ate the Chinese food and chips for supper and washed it down with Coke. Mike had not forgotten. Alan thanked him. He told him about the dirty oil in the tractor. Mike said he would get that next weekend when out. "Did you find anything else interesting, or were you too busy?" Mike asked.

Alan said he had been too busy, but wanted to look over the books in the library after supper. Mike had already started drinking. He mixed the bourbon with the Coke liberally and before long was in his usual condition in the evening, drunk. "I'm heading to bed early, Alan," Mike said. "I have not been feeling well."

Alan told him he needed to slow up on his drinking. Mike told him it wasn't that. He believed he was coming down with something. The next week Mike felt like he was only running at half power. Alan did most of the work that week. He finished up mixing the potting medium, filled all the plastic pots and placed them in the double wide trailer that was the size of a full size house.

That week Alan looked further into the many books of Mike's uncle. Most of them were about the French and Indian War in the local area. Two caught his interest, *Guns at the Forks* and *Braddock at the Monongahela*. Both were about General Braddock, his campaign against the French and Indians and his defeat in the wilderness near present day Pittsburgh, Pennsylvania. He remembered in grade school his class had gone on a field trip to Fort Frederick near Hancock, Maryland. The teacher told them how General Braddock's army traveled though there on its way to battle. After its defeat, Fort Frederick had been built to defend against invasion from the French and Indians coming from the West.

By Friday, Mike was sick as a dog. Friday night Mike stayed at the old house. He told Alan, "Tomorrow, I want you to take my truck to town and get groceries. I feel terrible. This has to be the flu bug. I've got a fever and I feel like I got hit by a bus, a big one."

The next morning Mike gave Alan the truck keys and a list of groceries to get. He also gave him some rough directions to the grocery store and then went back to bed. Alan hopped into Mike's truck and headed down the farm lane. As he stopped at the gate, an idea came to him. He would go to a hardware store and duplicate the truck keys and the gate key. Those two items could be very handy in the future. He drove down the road across the creek and soon was in the small, sleepy town of Patterson Creek. He could see a Volunteer Fire Department building, an old school, but no stores of any kind. Soon he was on the serpentine Old Furnace Road. He passed the Brethren Church across the road from the old iron furnace that gave the area and road its name.

Unsure of which way to go at the T-bone intersection, he pulled into the parking lot at Linda's Old Furnace Restaurant. He asked a patron leaving the restaurant the way to Cumberland and the man pointed the way. Alan thanked him. He stopped at the road for traffic to clear. There he saw the black and white West Virginia Historical Marker. It was nearly three feet by three feet. It was about Fort Sellers. *That name was familiar.* Quickly it came to him. He had seen that name in a book on West Virginia Indian forts in Uncle Michael's library. But if he remembered right, Fort Sellers had been somewhere around the town of Patterson Creek. He made a mental note to check on it later.

He pulled out on Route 28 and headed for Cumberland. The road twisted and turned a lot with only one long straight stretch suitable for passing before he reached Wiley Ford. He took a left there and headed for Ridgeley. The road was narrow with a mountain on one side and nothing on the other. There was no shoulder on either side and only an inadequate stretched wire guardrail on the steep side that dropped off rapidly and precariously. In Ridgeley, he slowed for an obvious speed trap. He continued at twenty-five miles an hour, rounded a bend, went under a railroad bridge, took another right, then a left. Another historical plaque stood on the left side of the road. It read "On this site, stood Fort Ohio, a block house and trading post built by the Ohio Company of which George Washington was a partner. Fort Ohio served Colonial and British troops and frontiersmen in the mid 1770s. After Fort Cumberland located across the river on the hill above Will's Creek was constructed, Fort Ohio slowly fell into disuse and was abandoned after the conclusion of the French and Indian War."

So this was where Fort Ohio was located and Fort Cumberland, too. He remembered those names from the books he looked at in the old farmhouse library. He pulled the truck back on the road and passed over the bridge across the Potomac River separating West Virginia from Maryland. Back in the

1700s there was no West Virginia, only Virginia. Separation came at the time of the American Civil War. He could thank his sixth grade teacher for that fact. As he waited for the light under the crosstown bridge that carried Interstate 68 to turn green, he saw a small log building in a little park by the road. A small plaque said, "George Washington's Headquarters during his stay at Fort Cumberland 17-- something or the other." Alan could not make that out. The numbers were obscured by something, probably pigeon poop. And then it continued, "moved to this location from the hill to the northwest, present site of the Cumberland Presbyterian Church."

The light turned green and Alan drove the truck forward. He took a left at the intersection and drove up the hill. He parked in front of the Allegany County Library, got out of the truck, and walked across the street. There he saw a life size statue of George Washington and numerous plaques about the various historical items that happened here. Walking down the street, he saw where a local group of historians put granite markers in the present street to show the location of old Fort Cumberland. He also saw a statue of British General Braddock. The plaque read, "From this spot, General Edward Braddock led his ill-fated army westward through the wilderness in spring of 1755. They were soundly defeated in the Battle of the Monongahela east of present day Pittsburgh, Pa. Their defeat left this area open to the ravaging attacks of the French and Indians. Many settlers were killed or carried off by the marauding savages."

Alan realized he needed to get going. He walked back to Mike's truck, drove it around the square where the court house sits, took a right down the road with the markers in it, and stopped at the foot of the hill at the sign. When it was clear, he pulled out and continued over Wills Creek. He saw the Western Maryland Railroad Depot used mainly by tourists today for the train rides up the mountain with the old coal-fired engine that billowed black smoke and cinders along the tracks. Here, a sign said the National Parks System had a museum on the C & O Canal. He pulled off Baltimore Street onto a side street. Luck was with him. He spied a hardware store and found a spot to park. Alan dropped the required coins into the meter and walked back to the store. There a clerk was happy to cut the keys Alan needed. Alan paid the fee, put the keys in his pocket, and walked out of the store. He was getting hungry and had seen a hot dog stand across the street from where he had parked. The sign read, "Coney Island, established 1918. When Johnnie went marching off to war, we were here." There was a silhouette of a WW I dough boy on the sign. Alan went in the store, was warmly greeted by a man he took to be the owner and shown a seat in a booth with high sides. A waitress took his order, two hot dogs with the special house topping she had recommended, a large order of French fries, and a root beer. As he was sitting there, he noticed two men, one white, and one black, sitting in the booth across from him. The old hatred from prison reared up in Alan. *Why did they have to let him in here?* he thought.

From their conversation, he could tell they were both men of the cloth. The white man's name was Tom and the black man he called Padre. It was hard to hear in the busy restaurant. The waitress brought Alan his food. It was good. He had been eating his own cooking for so long; anything different would and did taste good. The men's conversation continued with Alan still only catching pieces. Padre said something about vandalism at the church, but it was hard to hear with the background noise of the customers and the TV blasting news. The white man spoke in a quiet voice and Alan only caught two words that sounded like, "Braddock's Gold," but that was about all. They finished their meal and left. Alan did not get a good look at either of them. He finished eating and went to pay at the cash register.

The man there asked, "How was your meal?"

Alan said, "Great. This is the first time I've been here. I hope it's not the last."

The owner was pleased. "Glad you liked it. Come again."

Alan asked who were those two men who just left, the salt and pepper pair.

The owner said the black guy was a priest for the Catholic Church near Fort Ashby over on Route 28 and the white man ran a water bottling business in Short Gap. He said it was a real shame about the trouble they had at the Catholic Church. The vandals had messed up the church because of the black priest. He said he thought people were over that kind of stuff. It belonged in the old days and not today. Alan agreed with him to his face, but deep inside he burned. The man looked similar to the one who beat him up so badly in prison, but then Alan chucked to himself, *don't they all look alike?*

Perhaps he would pay the padre and his church a visit some night for fun. Alan paid the cashier, walked out the door and to the truck down the street. He drove the short distance through the streets of downtown Cumberland to the grocery store. There he found the items that were on Mike's list plus a few more. He also purchased a prepaid cell phone and an extra phone card. Alan did not know when he could get away from the farm again. He would tell Mike the phone was for calling his mother. Mike knew the rule about never using the phone the Voice had given for personal business. Alan paid for the groceries with the money Mike had given him. He used some of the money the Voice had provided for him to pay for the phone and an extra-prepaid minutes card. Soon he was back in the truck heading for the old farm high on the ridge above Patterson Creek. It had been an interesting day. Several opportunities had opened up for him today and several questions on local history had aroused a curiosity in him that needed answers. When he got back to the old house, he found Mike still sleeping. *He's probably has the flu. The rest will do him good.* Alan threw a TV dinner in the microwave and it was soon done. He sat it next to the books he had chosen from the library in the old house. He had questions that needed answers. Perhaps he would even find something interesting. His curiosity had been aroused.

Chapter 37

Alan rose early as usual. He sat on the old porch, drinking a cup of coffee. Looking at the sky, he remembered an old rhyme of his mother, "Red in the morn, sailors take warn. Red in the night, sailors delight." He found this more accurate than the weatherman. It was a bright red sky. That meant a good possibility of thunderstorms this time of year. Overall, the summer had been dry. The pot plants had been growing rapidly. Alan had checked on them this morning. No mice damage again. That stray cat had been busy. Before she came, the mice had been eating the tender plants. He and Mike were sitting on the porch when the skinny feline had first appeared. Mike had wanted Alan to shoot her, but he pointed out the cat might be useful with the mouse problem and so she was. Mike had agreed to that point. Though he bought the cat food, Mike never fed her or paid any attention to the cat. Alan had often wondered to himself if Mike would get rid of him and the cat when they were no longer needed. He still remembered the crack Mike had made about having to shoot him. This still bothered Alan.

"That cat's a female," Mike had said when he first saw the feline.

"And just how do you know that?" inquired Alan.

"All calico cats are female," he replied, "or at least all I've ever seen."

He was right. The poor cat had probably been dumped off by some heartless person, but she now had at home here. Mike never allowed her in the house.

Alan found the old gun Mike said was probably there. It had been up in the attic hidden under some insulation, along with a near-full box of shells. The small rifle was a Remington 223. Alan and Mike set up some tin cans out about 200 feet and shot at them. The gun was sited-in well and very accurate. Mike commented on Alan's accurate shooting. "You're a natural."

Alan claimed beginners luck, but after killing some night visitors, raccoons and possums, with one shot each, they knew he could handle a gun skillfully. "You keep the vermin cleaned outta here," Mike had said. "You're a good shot."

"I'll do that," Alan had responded. He wondered to himself if that included both two and four legged vermin.

Mike was still drinking heavily in the evening. Often in the morning, he was late getting up. "That stuff will ruin you," Alan had told him, but Mike had always shrugged it off.

Alan had been doing much reading in Uncle Michael's library. He noted how books on General Braddock's march, the old forts of this area, and the legend of Braddock's Gold kept turning up. Several books suggested the British payroll in gold had been hidden and then lost. Various locations in four states were suggested. Uncle Michael even kept a book of his personal notes on this. *Could this legend of lost gold be true? Not likely*, he thought, *but old Uncle Michael seemed to have taken it seriously*. He had some really obscure writings on this matter in his collection. More reading would have to wait. He could hear Mike up and looking for coffee in the kitchen. Another day of work was ahead. And it was going to be a hot one. The huge automatic fans that helped cool the trailer in the summer had already started. The large hoods directed the hot air through louvers toward the house. No one in the air would ever see the distinctive green of the marijuana. Many precautions had been taken to see this place remained a secret.

"Hey, you ready to go?" Alan heard Mike holler from the inside of the house.

"Yah, times a wastin'. Let's get crackin'," Alan replied.

Five minutes later, they were hard at work and Alan was right. It was a hot one that day. The days went quickly and routinely. The plants now were as tall as Alan. In about two weeks, they would touch the ceiling of the old trailer. At that time, they would be topped. This would encourage the side branches to fill out and the harvest would be greater. They could see the light at the end of the tunnel. Alan found some detailed local maps in Uncle Michael's library. He decided he needed a possible escape plan. Be prepared, just like the Boy Scouts said. He found a detailed service map on the Chesapeake & Ohio Canal National Park. The Park paralleled the Potomac from Cumberland, MD. to Washington, D.C. If he could make it to the canal, he could ride the bike to Hagerstown and Momma. One Saturday at sunrise while Mike was away, Alan rode the old bike down the hill and over the creek to the small town of Patterson Creek. He took the road to where it dead-ended at the twin railroad tracks that followed the Potomac. He stashed the bike in tall weeds, mainly tall ironweed with its purple flowers on top, goldenrod also in bloom and a little poison ivy. He walked down the tractor lane to the cornfield by the river. There, Alan looked at the spot that had been an old ford. It would be difficult but doable if he had to, if the waters didn't get higher from summer rainfall.

He went back and got his bike out of the tall weeds. There was a truck path along the railroad. If the highway map was accurate, about five miles downstream the railroad crossed the river and would be soon within a stone's throw of the old tow path, now used by hikers and walkers in the C & O Canal National Park. It was only about three miles to the bridge and the bridge also had room for a narrow road way for the railroad maintenance trucks. Alan waited for a southbound coal train to cross the bridge. He listened for another train coming, but he only heard the sound of birds and the wind. Alan quickly and carefully rode over the bridge. In approximately one half mile, the railroad crossed over the canal. This was not on the map.

Alan looked down at the towpath. The escape plan was possible and doable.

Satisfied, Alan turned around and headed back. He took his time. The only time he had been away from the old house, except for the time Alan went to town for groceries, was when Mike was sick. He enjoyed being away for a while. By now, he was back in the sleepy little town. A few kids were playing in the yards. Several women were putting out wash on the clotheslines and lawns were getting cut. He passed the barn on the road to the stream. Alan saw several pigs lying in their muddy wallows and some black cows. The wind was blowing the farm smells toward him. They were pretty strong. *Nothing like the smell of animals and manure,* thought Alan. Several young boys and their fathers were fishing in the creek. Alan stopped and watched one boy land a large fish. It looked like a small-mouthed bass. That would make some good eating. Alan rode to the hill, there he dismounted and walked the bike up the steep hill. He rode the bike to the gate that blocked the road to the old farmhouse. Alan used his new key to open the gate and went in. He locked the gate behind him and rode the last stretch to the house. After putting the bike away, he checked on the marijuana. The pots were getting a little dry, but that was the plan. A little dryness would help kill pathogens that could harm the crop and it would extend the water supply from the well. The well had no problems so far. A dry well would be a disaster. Mike was concerned of this possibility and the men were using the water at the house carefully.

Alan fixed a bowl of vegetable beef soup and threw in a hand full of oyster crackers. He ate heartily. It had been a strenuous day. He washed it down with some orange Gatorade. He had just finished washing his dishes, when he heard Mike drive up. Alan walked to the front door and opened the screen door. A fly came into the house. Mike was out of the truck and heading for the house. And he was drunk, very drunk. His drinking had been bad as of late. He stumbled toward Alan.

"How you doin'?" Mike slurred.

"Okay, Mike, Okay. Mike you're drunk," Alan said.

Mike smiled silly from ear to ear, "Yup," he agreed.

Alan decided right then and there something must be done. But Mike was in no condition for a serious talking to now. Alan knew this from dealing with his own Dad.

Mike staggered past Alan and into the house. There he fell over the cheap expandable coffee table in the living room. It broke in two with a loud crash. Mike lay on the broken item. Slowly he got up. "I'm okay, I'm okay," he said. Alan grabbed Mike by the arm to steady him. He helped him to his room.

"Mike, we need to talk, tomorrow," Alan said.

"Okay," was all he replied before he collapsed on the bed and fell asleep.

Alan was pretty disgusted, but he would save his lecture for Mike until he was sober tomorrow. He went out to the living room and looked at the two broken halves of the table. This he would use as a prop in his lecture to Mike. Alan moved the pieces to the side of the room. On one side of the louvers he noted a piece of electrical tape. When the table was together he had not seen this. *Strange*, he thought. He pulled off the tape. Alan saw the shiny edge of what looked like a coin. He pulled the hidden item out of a hidden slot and looked at it. It was a coin, an old coin. Where had he seen this before? Like a flash, it came to him. This coin looked like the picture of a guinea coin in the book about Braddock's Gold. He checked in the book. It was. It was a coin like Braddock had carried in his lost payroll. *Why, that sly old fox,* Alan thought. *Uncle Michael had a piece of Braddock's Gold. It really did exist, but where was the rest? Where did he get this and when? What else had Uncle Michael hidden here besides the gun and this coin? The irony of it. I would never have found this if old drunk Mike hadn't fallen over the coffee table.* Alan put the coin in his front left pants pocket. He would keep it here for safekeeping. It had been an interesting day. He had learned much, but many new questions had arrived. Questions that needed to be answered, but now he was tired. Tomorrow was another day and the questions could wait until then. Alan took a quick shower and checked on Mike. He was snoring loudly. Alan shut the bedroom door and went to his room. Soon he was asleep and dreaming of riches, ... gold, ... Braddock's Gold.

Chapter 38

Alan woke the next morning feeling refreshed. He had new hope. If this endeavor with the Voice didn't work out, he had an option. Perhaps he would not need Mike or the Voice if he could find Braddock's Gold. He knew he, just like the man in the red shirt on Star Trek, was expendable if necessary. Uncle Michael had been hot on its trail and now, Alan had evidence it was real. One book identified the man on the coin as British King Charles II. The coin had three ounces of gold in it. Another book had suggested the gold payroll was in Spanish doubloons, pieces of eight, but why would an English King want or need to use Spanish coins when he could mint his own? That didn't make any sense to Alan, but stranger things had happened.

He fixed the last of the eggs and bacon for breakfast. He used the last of the salsa, too. Mike had not been to the store as usual. Alan checked the truck for the weekly supplies. There was none, which was probably a good thing. Alan hated to think what a man in Mike's drunken condition might have done at the grocery store. His mere presence could have created a bad situation. They did not need to bring attention to themselves.

Alan walked out of the house and headed to the old double wide to check on the illegal crop. The mouse population was practically nil since the cat had arrived. The grass was getting high and needed mowing. From out to the green jungle, a black racer snake zipped across the path. Alan was startled and jumped. The snake disappeared into the weeds. "Better cut the grass today," Alan mumbled aloud to himself. As an after thought, he added, "And the big field in front of the house."

The snake was another reason the mice had been disappearing. Alan did not like snakes, but tolerated them for their benefits, though he had killed several rattlers while he resided at the old house. He recovered his composure and walked the rest of the way to the grow house. Inside he checked on the moisture level in the pots. They were getting dry. He checked the fertilizer injection bucket. It needed more which he added along with a little fungicide. Next, he turned the automatic watering back on and the liquid with the blue color from the fertilizer started trickling out of the spaghetti-like drip irrigation lines. Mike told him they were developed in Israel to save precious water in that dry land.

The plants were growing tall and harvest time was nearing. This was not a time to make an error. The temperature in the building seemed right in spite of the heat from the grow lights. All was well. He left and headed for the house. He walked carefully and looked for the snake, but he was gone. Alan went around the corner and saw Mike sitting on the porch. His hair was uncombed and he was smoking a cigarette. He looked pretty rough. Alan thought his mother would have described his look as being *like something the cat drug in*. Mike looked up at Alan and then dropped his eyes. Alan continued to the porch. "How are you this morning?" Alan asked.

"Not so good," Mike replied. "I feel like I got hit by a Greyhound Bus. What happened to the coffee table?"

"Mike, you were drunk, drunk as a skunk, last night when you came in," Alan said. "You had no business driving in that condition. And you fell over the coffee table. You broke it in two. I had to pick you up and carry you to bed. You were wasted. Your drinking has gotten out of hand. What would have happened if you got in a wreck or got picked up on a DWI? What would I have done if you didn't show up? Call the Voice and try to explain the situation? That would have gone over like a lead balloon."

With the mention of the Voice, Mike stiffened and a startled look occupied his face. Alan could see he had his attention. Alan continued, "I'm not saying you need to go cold turkey. My dad did and he got the DT's. It was *not* a pretty picture. Mike, you got to cut down on your drinkin'. You're endangering this whole operation. From what you have told me about this Voice guy, I wouldn't want to be around when he gets bad news."

Mike sat there with that same shocked look on his face. His eyes caught Alan's. "You're right. My drinkin' is out of hand. And no way do you ever want to disappoint the Voice. It just ain't healthy."

Over the next week, Mike still drank, but only in the evening and never to excess. Alan breathed a sigh of relief. They made do with what groceries they had at the house. Some of the meals would be kind of funky, but they would get by. Alan cut the grass by the house and in the field with the tractor. He noted the strange pattern in the field around where the old sycamore tree had been. It seemed like a square about 100 feet on each side. He wondered what could have made that pattern. It was a mystery.

The following Saturday with Mike away, Alan searched the old house throughout. *What else had Uncle Michael hidden?* He checked the attic and found nothing. He had the same results with the search of the tractor shed. He looked the house over closely, but again found nothing new.

Alan got a tall glass of iced tea from the refrigerator. It was unsweetened. He never had liked the super sweet tea that was a standard for the area. He sat in the chair at the desk by the bookcase that held the collection of Uncle Michael. *Just where would the old guy hide important information,* Alan asked himself, *just where?* Alan sat for a minute looking at the books. An anomaly caught his alert eyes. The seemingly symmetric bookcase was just so slightly different at the bottom right hand. Alan looked closely.

He took the books off the bottom shelf. Unlike the others, this shelf was not nailed down. The wood case had been routed out to receive this shelf and only this shelf. It was in snug and tight, but with a little pull, it came out. Hidden inside was a cigar box. Alan lifted it out and opened it. Inside he found clipping from newspapers and photocopied articles. All were about Braddock's Gold. Some were about where people believed it was hidden. There were various opinions that covered possible burial sites in four states around the old farm, but most seemed to center on West Virginia and Pennsylvania. Uncle Michael had written some notes in the margins. He seemed to believe the treasure, or a part of it, was buried somewhere right here in Mineral County. This was where the search was leading Alan. He pulled the rest of the papers from the box. There, taped to the bottom was a coin, a gold coin. It was in a sleeve. There was writing on the paper. It was the handwriting Alan could now recognize as belonging to Uncle Michael. And it said "Braddock's Gold 1994." It was for real. Uncle Michael had somehow found some of it.

He sat all this on the desk. Alan reached back down into the hiding place. He pulled out a brown shipping envelope with what seemed to contain a book. He reached in and pulled out a small hardback. He recognized the publisher. It was a vanity printing. The author had paid to have it printed. Alan open the front cover and read the handwriting on the inside page. It read "Michael, good luck with your hunt for Braddock's Gold. It's there and it will be found." Ira Ronald Lyon. 1994

He turned the page to the title page. It read, "The Quest for Braddock's Gold." The sub title read, "It WILL be found in our lifetime," by I. R. Lyon. Alan quickly skimmed through the slim book. It contained the story of Braddock's March into Pennsylvania, the battle where he and his army were defeated by the French and Indians, the retreat, and the loss of the payroll in gold coin. He told of various tales about what had become of the treasure that he believed had a value of somewhere between a half million to one million dollars today. Mr. Lyon gave the pros and cons of where he thought the gold was hidden. But he also stated he believed beyond the shadow of a doubt, the gold was hidden on the sites of the old French and Indian War forts in Mineral County, West Virginia.

Unfortunately, the locations of many of the West Virginia forts had been lost. George Washington could not locate Fort Cox in the late 1700s when he traveled through the area and he had visited it many times before it fell into disrepair. Lyon stated he could not and would not give up his source(s). On the last page of the book, he placed his home address in Fort Ashby, WV, his telephone number and invited anyone that wanted to share information on Braddock's Gold to contact him. Alan sat the book down and thought. Then he picked out another book from the shelf, one by William H. Ansel, Jr., called *Frontier Forts of the Potomac and Its Tributaries*. Alan thumbed the pages to Fort Sellers. He read these details, "A small fort located near the mouth of Patterson Creek about the same size as Fort Ashby." He remembered from the brochure in Uncle Michael's collection on Ashby's Fort and Museum that its dimensions were ninety feet by ninety feet. A satisfied smile came to his face. Alan knew he knew where Fort Sellers was.

He walked out to the new cut field to the odd square pattern. He had found Fort Sellers. It was up on this defensible hill, not down below like the book believed. Washington had directed it to be built up here. He had remembered this location from his surveying trip with Lord Fairfax when he was sixteen. Somewhere buried around here was a lot of gold and he wanted it. A plan was coming together.

He walked backed to the house and picked the book back up. He turned to the last pages. On the inside back cover was hand written the name, 'Tom Kenney,' Sons of American Revolution and a phone number. Alan knew he may need this. He wrote this on a small piece of paper and slipped it in his pocket. He remembered also seeing this name in one of Uncle Michael's books written in the margin.

Alan decided he would call Mr. Lyon. He dialed the phone number. The phone rang twice and a male voice answered "Hello?"

"Is this Mr. Lyon?" Alan asked.

"Yes, it is. Can I help you?" the male voice asked.

"Yes, sir, you can. I have your book on Braddock's Gold and I'd like to ask you some questions," Alan responded. "I saw your invitation to call and talk."

"I'm afraid I'm going to have to disappoint you, young man," the male voice said. 'I'm Ronald Lyon. You're looking for my father Ira Lyon. He died two weeks ago. He had lung cancer from years of smoking."

Alan expressed his sympathy of the man's passing to his son. Ronald told him the hunt for Braddock's Gold had been father's passion, not his. The extent of his knowledge was from what he had read in the father's book and he could be of no more help to him. Alan thanked him for his time and help. He hung up. He returned the book and cigar box to the hiding place and then put the other books back as they had been. He would sleep on all this new information, but he had a pretty good idea of what he needed to do already. Soon Mike would be back. Alan hoped he would be sober. He was and had groceries. The evening went quickly. Alan slept well that night.

In another location, a person known as the Voice wondered about the goings-on in an old farmhouse above the sleepy little town of Patterson Creek. And he did not like to be disappointed.

Chapter 39

It was Monday morning. Tom tried to find a fishing partner, but none were available. The Padre declined saying he was off for personal business in the Pittsburgh area. His sons were busy with their business and wanted Tom to help. He said no. The boss could do what he wanted and he wanted to go fishing. So off he went. He drove down the Old Furnace Road to the town of Patterson Creek and through the quiet dell to where the road dead-ended at the railroad tracks. Tom parked there out of the way, got his fishing pole and his tackle box, walked over the railroad tracks and down the tractor lane to the cornfield that occupied the bottom line by the river. *I wonder what's biting today and on what?* he thought.

The old Potomac River had become so much cleaner since the big dam had been put in upsteam near the headwaters. Tom threw the worm baited hook into a deep pool. He got a bite soon afterward and pulled in the first of three big catfish he would get there. They averaged about sixteen inches long. After that, the river went dead. Nothing was biting. Tom decided to try somewhere else. He walked up to the old truck and put the catfish on the ice in his cooler in the bed of the truck. Tom downed a cool bottle of water, Knobley Mountain of course. He hopped in the old truck, spun it around, and was soon over the low water bridge on Patterson Creek. He parked just on the other side. Within a minute, he was wetting a line in the pool above the bridge.

Fifteen minutes later, he had two bass, one about twelve inches, and the other approximately two inches longer. He fished another thirty minutes, but the creek had gone dead for Tom. So it was back to the truck, put the new fish on ice and back on the road again. He drove up the hill and the road took a sharp right. He traveled another three miles and there Dans Run Road paralleled the Potomac. Tom found a place to park and grabbed his gear again. He waited for a passing freight train, crossed the tracks and walked the short distance to the river. He caught two huge carp and threw the trash fish up on the bank to die. Tom knew they tasted like mud. Joann had cooked one for him early in their marriage and it was awful. He reassured her that it wasn't her cooking. It was usually great, fit for a king. He caught one more carp, the biggest yet, and threw it up with the others. *Nothing but carp here* he thought. He grabbed his equipment and headed for the truck. By the time he reached it, he decided to continue on up Dans Run Road to Fort Ashby. He had several overdue books to return to the library.

He passed the goat farm on the right. They looked like meat goats to him. He did not see any udders for milk on them. At a fork in the road, he took a right. The left fork took you to Middle Ridge over Indian Hollow Road. He had been told that area was the site of an old Indian village. The farmers were always plowing up artifacts there he heard. He went by the Wagoner's National Bicentennial Farm and earth-sheltered underground house. It faced south for maximum usage of the sun's warming rays during the winter. In the summer, the deciduous trees shaded the exposed south side. Tom figured their monthly fuel bills must be next to nothing. He drove past the church at the corner of Dennison Hollow Road and Dans Run Road. On his right he spotted a crude, hand written sign that read, 'Large Brown Eggs, $1.50 dz'. He looked up the lane to the old weathered farmhouse. The roof was good, but the white painted bricks needed paint years ago. There was only a white hint of paint still covering the red brick. The porch was in bad shape and vines grew up the house. Tom knew this place. Dan Phares lived here. Tom had gone to school with Dan. Dan was autistic and he had a younger brother. When their parents died, Dan got a life estate in the old house, and the brother got the farm, with the stipulation that the younger brother was to see Dan was provided for. The barns on the farm looked well cared for, but the old house looked very run down. Tom drove up the steep farm lane to the house that sat on the south end of Patterson Creek Ridge. Tom could see up the valley into Fort Ashby. Down to the right, he noticed Timmy Miltenberger playing by the cottage surrounded by the tall limbless silver maples and sycamores that he called home by Patterson Creek.

"Hello," he heard a voice shout. "Hello, need some eggs?"

Tom turned around and saw Dan Phares standing on the porch of the house. Dan was a sight. He never looked you in the eye, always to the side, and he held one arm, the left one always drawn up to his chest. His looks scared many people, but Tom knew him from childhood.

"Oh, it's you, Tom," said Dan. "You here for eggs or something else? I got plenty. Business hasn't been good lately. And they're from free-range chickens, too."

"Yah, I'll take a dozen," Tom said. "How you been, Dan? I haven't seen you in a while. It doesn't look like your brother is taking good care of the house."

Dan replied, "What's wrong with it? It's just like I want it. I got all I need, a roof over my head, clothes, and wood for the stove to cook and keep warm. I can't think of much more that I would want."

"I see your point," Tom said. "You have everything you need to be happy."

"That's right," Dan replied. "Tom, I knew you'd understand. Back when we were in school, you never picked on me or called me names just because I was different. You were always kind to me."

"That's how I was raised," Tom said. "My folks always told me to treat everyone with kindness, the old Golden Rule you know."

Dan shook his head yes. "You still want them eggs?"

Tom said yes and Dan motioned for Tom to follow him. He did. They went to the east side of the house where the entrance to the cellar was and went in. It was cool, damp, and dark. Dan pulled a string and a naked incandescent lit up. "There they are," he said and pointed to the brown eggs.

Dan put the eggs in a carton and handed them to Tom. Tom took two dollars from his wallet and handed them to Dan. He reached into his pocket with his one good hand and dropped two shiny coins into Tom's waiting hand. Tom looked at the coins. One was a normal silver Jefferson quarter. The other one was golden in color. Tom looked at it closely. It was exactly like the one the Padre had shown him. Tom held the gold coin up between his thumb and fore finger. He asked, "Where did you get this?"

Dan looked at the coin and grimaced. "That's my lucky coin. Can I have it back? I'll give you another quarter."

"Where did you get this?" Tom asked.

Dan replied, "I'll tell you because you are my friend, Tom. They've been in my family for a long, long time. That's what Daddy told me. He said they were valuable. It's all in that old book there on the shelf. I sell one every now and then to a guy who has a shop in Cumberland. He gives me lots of money for one. It lasts a long time."

Tom asked, "Can I see the book?"

"Sure," Dan replied. "I think I lost one last year. I think I gave it in change to a guy I sold eggs to. He didn't give it back. I didn't notice till he was gone. I think he said his name was Michael."

Tom took the book and read. It was hand written by someone that was barely literate. It was a story of how he had been one of the men that had buried Braddock's Gold in Pennsylvania. He had escaped the massacre. After the last Indian war in this area in 1763, he had settled this homestead and gone back for the gold. He feared it would be discovered here, so he hid it in the old abandoned frontier forts of the area. The gold was placed in swivel guns and buried. To mark the spot, he planted a buttonwood tree. And his name was John Phares.

Tom looked at Dan. "This book is very important. Don't show it to anyone. Evil people would do anything to have the information in the book. Tell no one, ever."

For once, Dan looked straight at Tom. "Okay, Tom, I trust you. You know what's best. I won't show it to nobody."

"Promise?" Tom asked.

"Yup, promise. Cross my heart and hope to die," Dan said seriously.

They walked out of the cellar and to Tom's truck. Tom got in and started it up. Dan was standing by the truck. Tom said, "Thanks for the eggs. They will make a great omelet. And remember tell no one and don't show that gold coin around. Take care of yourself, Dan. I need to stop more often."

"You do that and I'll do what you say. See ya later alligator," Dan said.

To which Tom responded, "After while crocodile."

And off he went down the lane to the main road into Fort Ashby. Information like this could be dangerous. He hoped Dan would follow his advice. He wondered what he should do with this knowledge, if anything. He hardly noticed any of the road till he got to the old fort. He looked up the hill to the cemetery where Brian was buried. Tom said a little prayer, "Dear God, take care of my son and give me the wisdom to know what to do with this information."

He turned the corner at the square onto Route 28. The air was getting cooler. It was the first hint of the upcoming winter and it would be here soon, way too soon. Tom paid the fine for the overdue books at the library and headed for home. He had fish to clean and a business to check on. His sons should have been able to keep things steady for the day. And what would he do with this burdensome new information? *Lord, give me wisdom.*

Chapter 40

Alan was feeling very anxious and stressed as he sat on the porch of the old house. His mother had called his cell phone. It had been off. Her message said his dad had beaten her up again. *Damn that SOB. damn him to hell.* He wanted so much to rescue his mom and little brother but how? The answer was here somewhere, hidden. The grow house marijuana was almost ready for harvest. *Would the Voice give him his share of the profit from the operation or not?* Alan could not forget the crack Mike had made about maybe having to kill him at the start of this. Would he get his cut or would he find his reward for services rendered was a bullet to the head? He was afraid. He did not want to die alone on some remote hillside in West Virginia. The gold was here somewhere. He knew it. He could feel it. If he found it, he could take the old bike, fill the baskets with the gold, and ride to the railroad down by the Potomac at the mouth of Patterson Creek. He would travel along it until he got to the old towpath on the C & O National Park and from there, he would take the towpath to Hagerstown. A gold dealer would buy some of the gold. He'd rent a car, rescue his mom and brother, and head for somewhere no one could find them. That was the plan, a shaky one at best, but better than none at all.

Mike came out the front door and said, "I'll be leaving now. I should be back late Sunday. The Voice says he needs me for the weekend."

Mike had left like this before and always returned when he said he would.

With that, he was off. Alan watched the truck get smaller as it rolled down the farm lane. Half aloud, he said to himself, "Yah, he'll probably give you instructions on the harvest and how he wants my body disposed of."

Alan had concluded from the old books and papers that Mike's uncle accumulated that the gold, Braddock's Gold, or at least a large portion of it was somewhere here on the farm, but where? He was missing a piece of the puzzle. One old book claimed it was buried at Fort Sellers and he now knew he had found the fort right in the field in front of the house. Two weeks ago, he noticed the odd lines the plants made in the field. The lines formed a box with diamond patterns at the corners. It was the shape of old Fort Sellers. It was not out at Old Furnace like the Historical Sign indicated, but right here under his feet. There were some handwritten notes from Mike's uncle indicating somewhere he had found information that placed the gold on this farm, but the page with the exact location was missing. Alan was getting desperate. The only thing else he had in the notes was a name and phone number. It belonged to a Tom Kenney. *Who was he? Did he know where the gold was or not?* Alan decided he would risk calling him.

It was a slow morning at the Knobley Mountain Bottled Water office. The drivers were out on deliveries. Tom and his son were at their desks doing some paperwork. Tom was exasperated. He let out a loud sigh and said to Doug, "Will there ever be an end to this new government paperwork?"

"Not till the next election," Doug said. "That clown in the White House and his gang on Capitol Hill never ran a business. If they did, I'm sure they'd crash and burn really quick. They don't have a clue what it takes to be successful in running a business, or a county!"

"Hey, Doug, get the phone," requested Tom. "We've got a call. I smell money."

Doug picked up the receiver. "Hello, Knobley Mountain Bottled Water. How can we help you? Okay. Dad, it's for you." Doug held his hand over the receiver on the phone.

"Who is it, Doug?"

"He wouldn't say. Just says he needs to talk to you."

"Okay," Tom grabbed his desk phone. "Hello, this is Tom Kenney. How can I help you? What? Why, yes, really? Yes, I think I can help. How do I get there? Yes. Okay. That's left at the gate? Okay, see you soon. Bye."

"What was all about Dad?" asked Doug.

"Some guy named Alan Grey says he's found old Fort Seller down at Patterson Creek, the town of, that is. Says he found my name and phone number in some notes of his roommate's late Uncle Michael Levy. I think we are about to make an important discovery. I think I know where on his farm Braddock's lost gold is located."

"Dad, come on. This sounds like another wild goose chase. You told me that was just an old wive's tale," said Doug.

"I used to think it was till I bought some eggs," replied Tom. "Now I believe we are on to something big."

"Okay, Pop," Doug said. "Go off and play and leave me to mind the shop."

"You are probably right," he paused, "but I'm still going. That's one of the advantages of being the senior partner in this outfit," said Tom.

Doug rolled his eyes. "Okay, Popster, get going."

"But first, a trip to the bathroom."

"Why did I know that, why?" laughingly questioned Doug.

"Old guy rule number 1," replied Tom. "Never pass up a bathroom."

Doug just shook his head. He went back to work at the desk. Another call came in and he took it. A minute later Tom walked back through the office and out the door. Doug heard his dad's truck start up and off he went. Doug glanced over at Tom's desk. He noted the crude map of directions Tom had drawn was still on the desk. *He'll be back if he couldn't remember them,* thought Doug. *He'll be back.*

Tom traveled two miles north on WV Route 28. It was at that point he remembered the directions. *No, he wasn't going back. He could remember them.* Down the crooked Old Furnace Road he went. He took a left on the road to the sleepy town of Patterson Creek. Once there he turned right on the unmarked road that led to the low water bridge over Patterson Creek, the stream. He followed the road up the hill and soon found the gate that blocked the road up to the old farmhouse where Alan waited. The chain was dummy-locked just as Alan had said. Tom shut the gate behind him. *Was this going to be worth his while or just another disappointment as Doug expected?* He would soon know.

Chapter 41

Mike stopped the truck at the gate to the main road. He unlocked it, drove through and locked it again. He wondered what the special job was that the Voice had summoned him for. *Just like the Voice* he thought, *everything you need to know and less*. Still, the Voice had treated him well over the years. He slowed for the low water bridge. That's a beautiful view. Soon he was on the serpentine Old Furnace Road. He had heard the engineers in WV who laid out the roads had been paid by the mile and this road seemed a testimony of that. He pulled into the parking lot that served the Old Furnace Restaurant, better known as Linda's, and the grocery store. He went in and purchased a soda, chips, and some gum, cinnamon. As he walked out the door, he noticed the black and white historical sign along Route 28. It was for Fort Sellers, the old fort that was active during the French and Indian war. Mike thought Uncle Michael was sure interested in all that ancient Colonial war stuff though he couldn't image why. History just didn't interest him, but Alan had sure taken to Uncle's old books. That was good. It would keep his mind active and him out of trouble.

Mike pulled the truck out on the Route 28 and headed for Cumberland. There he picked up Interstate 68 going east. He went past Rocky Gap State Park and over two mountains, Polish and Martin's. Soon the road joined I 70 E. Forty minutes later he passed Hagerstown. He noted the road sign, 17 miles to Antietam-Sharpsburg National Battlefield. This area was so full of history, the French and Indian War, American Revolution and the Civil War, but that interested Mike only a little. He neared the top of the second hill before Frederick. He went under the footbridge where the Appalachian Trail crossed the interstate and pulled into the rest stop just past it. Here he remembered the D.C. sniper had been caught. *Nut case*, Mike thought. *Why did he kill people without a reason?*

Just then his cell phone rang. "Hello?" he answered.

"Mike." It was the Voice, "There's been a change of plans, I won't be needing you."

"Understood, there's been a change of plans, I'm not needed today," said Mike.

"That is correct, Have a nice day," the Voice replied. Then click, the line went dead.

Mike thought, *that's so like the Voice, to the point, then gone. "Have a nice day," what a guy, this Voice. I guess I have the day off and can go back to the house, but then, Saturday was the day I usually visited Flossy, I'd just be early.* Mike could see her in the stewardess outfit, fly the friendly skies united, as they had many times.

After using the facilities at the rest stop, he grabbed a Maryland state tourist book and headed to the truck. What luck, ten minutes from the rendezvous point and the job for him was canceled. *Have a nice day. I will.* So he turned the truck around at the next exit and headed for Ned's Place and Flossy.

Before long, Mike was back to Hagerstown. Three minutes later, he pulled into the empty parking lot of the bar. Ned's Place, Drink Old German Beer, said the sign out front. He got out of the truck and walked to the front door. There was a closed sign on it. He tried the door. It was unlocked and he went in. Mike heard a male voice, "Sorry, we're closed."

A tall, big man came in the room. "Mike, what are you doing here?" The big man asked. "You usually don't get here till later."

"Well, there was a change of plans and I was in the neighborhood," Mike said, "so I decided to stop in to see Belle and the girls."

"Okay," replied the big man. "Go right on back, you know the way."

Mike walked through the door marked 'Private,' turned left and stopped at the door with the buzzer and intercom. A closed circuit camera was on the wall watching. He rang the buzzer and waited. Soon a female voice said, "Why, Mike come on in." Mike heard the door click open and he went in the room. There stood Belle, the Madame. "Mike, I know why you're here, but why are you so early?"

"Change of plans," he said. "Where's Flossy?"

"I hate to disappoint you, Mike, but there was a death in her family, and she won't be back till Tuesday."

Belle read the disappointment on his face. "But Mike, I've got lots of other girls here to meet your every need."

"No, I don't think so," Mike said. "Me and Flossy kinda got a thing goin' on, if you know what I mean."

"Yah, I know what you mean," said Belle, "but I've got lots of other girls here that can make you happy. I know they can take care of your fantasies."

"No, I don't think so," replied Mike. "It just wouldn't be the same. Just tell her I was here and I will see her next weekend at the usual time."

"Okay, Mike," said Belle. "I'll pass that on to her when she gets back. Take care of yourself. See you next week."

After that Mike left the bar, got in his truck and got back on the interstate. *Well,* he thought. *If I can't get that need satisfied, I'll at least get me a good meal.*

Soon he was sitting at the Park and Dine Restaurant in Hancock, eating a hot turkey sandwich smothered in brown gravy, and washing it down with a cup of coffee, black. And it was all good. He thought, *got one of my basic needs satisfied.*

Before long, he was turning off of I 70 onto I 68 toward Cumberland. He passed by the welcome center at Sideling Hill with its displays and information of the geology of the area. *Someday I should stop there,* he thought, but this wasn't the day.

He stopped for gas in Flintstone and thirty minutes later he was crossing the C & O Canal in south Cumberland. Then he crossed the Wiley Ford bridge back into West Virginia and 15 minutes later he pulled up to the gate of the old house he called home now. He got out to unlock the gate, but found it already unlocked. *I must be slipping,* he thought. He drove through the gate and then locked it behind him. *This has been one crazy day* he thought. *I wonder how the rest of it will work out?* And he started the drive up the country lane to the farmhouse.

Chapter 42

Alan could not believe his luck. Mike would be gone all weekend. He could get a big head start on his plan of escape from the Voice and his minions. He could get his Momma and little brother and be long gone before they knew what had happened. By then, the trail would be cold. Alan would get the missing information on the gold's location out of Tom, tie him up, and use his vehicle for his escape. It was about time his luck changed. He opened the little trap door that went to the crawl space in the attic. There he found the .223 Remington rifle and a half box of ammo that Uncle Michael had hidden. He took it out of the old carrying case and loaded it. Alan hoped he would not have to use the gun, but he needed it to make sure he had Tom's full cooperation. He hid the weapon in his room till he needed it. Then he made a pot of coffee. He had to be a good host. Alan went out on the porch and waited. He saw the spider waiting patiently on her web. Two wasps wrapped in her silk hung from the web. Soon she would suck the life out of them. "Stupid spider," he mumbled to himself.

About ten minutes later Tom's old Chevy truck came up the farm lane and stopped in front of the house. Alan rose to his feet from the old chair and greeted his guest.

"Hello, I guess you're Tom, the Tom Kenney I just talked to?"

Tom replied, "That's right and you must be Alan?"

Alan nodded and said, "That is correct," as they shook hands.

"Have a seat," Alan said. "Would you like coffee?"

"Yes, I take mine black," answered Tom.

Alan left and returned with two cups of coffee. He gave one to Tom who thanked him for it.

Alan said, "I'm excited about this. I know I've found Fort Seller. It's right out there in the field. Look at the odd grass pattern. See the box shape about 100 feet square? That's where the walls were. And look at each point of the square. See a smaller diamond sticking out there? Can you see it?"

Tom strained his eyes. He looked in the area Alan was pointing. "No, I don't. Can you show me?"

"Sure," said Alan. "Come with me."

They got up from the chairs. Tom followed Alan into the field. Alan stopped at a slightly darker spot of grass. "Let me walk it out for you. Here is the bastion. See it?"

Then Alan walked about 100 feet in a straight line. "And here was a wall. There is another bastion here."

Alan made a ninety degree turn to the right and walked another 100 feet or so. "Here was another wall and another bastion on this corner. Can you see it yet?"

Tom shook his head no. Alan took another right angle turn and walked another 100 feet. Alan eagerly asked, "Can you see it yet?"

Tom said nothing. He studied the boxed area Alan had walked. *Was he on just another wild goose chase after an old tale that just would not die?* He stepped forward and rocked his shoulders from side to side to see things not as a flat picture, but in 3 D. Slowly his eyes began to see the difference in the grass color caused by the old wooden timbers buried in the ground. Yes, there it was—the old fort, Fort Seller. Tom began to visualize the walls and bastions. In his mind's eye, he even could see a few Colonial soldiers going about their daily chores.

Tom smiled. "Yes, I see it. I can see it now. There's the walls," and he pointed. "And right here where I am standing was a corner bastion," and with his finger he drew it out.

"That's it! You can see it!" Alan cried. "I really did find it! Wow!" and with that he did a little victory dance.

Tom was impressed. "Yes, you found it. This is quite an achievement. This location had been lost for more than 200 plus years. Now I bet you would like to find the gold if it's still here?"

"You betcha, the sooner the better. I can't wait," Alan said eagerly.

"My sources tell me the gold was buried in a swivel gun somewhere here at the old fort."

"A swivel gun?" Alan questioned. "What was a swivel gun and what did it look like?"

Tom started, "A swivel gun was a small frontier cannon used as an antipersonnel weapon. They were made of brass or iron. There were very few brass ones made. They were too expensive. They even had budget problems back then. The few left are in museums."

"How big were they?" Alan asked.

Tom replied, "About three feet long and about six inches in diameter."

"Are there any iron ones left?" Alan inquired.

"Very few, iron rusts away over the years," Tom replied.

"What would one of those left in the ground all these years look like today?" Alan asked.

"Like a piece of junk," Tom answered.

Alan questioned, "Like a rusty old pipe?"

"Yes, have you seen something like that here?" asked Tom.

Alan nodded. "Come with me."

They walked to the house. Alan told Tom to wait outside. He had something to show him. He would be right back.

Alan could not believe how things were falling into place. He knew where the gold was and soon he could take his Momma away. They would escape and start over somewhere new. Alan got the gun and walked out the front door. He pointed the gun at Tom and said, "Come with me," in the best commanding voice he could conjure up.

Tom's eyes grew big. "Whoa, now! No need for guns."

"Shut up, do what I say and no one gets hurt, understand?" Alan growled. "Get that shovel and come with me."

Tom did so and Alan walked him around the two old trailers. They continued over to the edge of the bank. Alan motioned down to the grave like pit where the old swivel gun lay buried. Just past the pit were the cliffs that protected this site and below that were the two sets of well-used railroad tracks.

"Get in that hole and dig," commanded Alan.

Tom looked at the grave shaped hole about three feet deep. "Are you going to kill me?"

"Dig," was all Alan said and he motioned Tom to the hole.

Tom walked to the hole, looked in it, and then jumped in. *So this is how I die,* thought Tom. He had not seen it coming. *How long would it be before they found my body? Would they find my body?* He began to dig through the trash and dirt.

At about this time Mike was pulling up to the gate to the farmhouse. He found it unlocked. *Strange* he thought, *I knew I locked that.* He drove up to the farmhouse and saw the strange truck. As he neared it, a long east bound coal train destined for a powerhouse rolled noisily toward the scene. Mike saw Alan standing at the cliff bank with his back to him. And he could tell he was carrying a rifle. Something was definitely wrong. Mike got out of the truck and walked around the trailers. He had his pistol in his hand. The coal train roared loudly by below. He called out, "Alan!"

Startled, Alan swung around and fired the rifle as he turned toward the shout. The bullet from the .223 Remington caught Mike in the rib case. As it was designed, it tumbled through his body, and he fell still to the ground. Alan turned the gun back toward Tom. "Dig," was all he said to Tom.

Tom went back to digging. He knew he was going to die. The noise from the eastbound train faded into the distance. He looked up at Alan and the gun. "Son, it doesn't have to end like this," he pleaded.

"Dig," Alan said and Tom did. From the east, the sound of another train came. It carried limestone and freight. It whistled as it neared the little used farm crossing. The noise from the train grew louder. Then two shots rang out. Tom looked up from the hole. Alan fell to the ground and did not move. Mike walked over and looked down at Alan. He was bleeding heavily from his wound. He looked at Tom and said, "I thought I might have to kill him."

With that, he pointed the gun at Tom and fired one shot at his head. Tom fell into the hole and lay still. Satisfied Tom was dead, Mike staggered ten feet forward toward the old farmhouse, stopped, went to his knees, and fell to the ground never to rise again.

Chapter 43

It was a beautiful day in Mineral County, West Virginia. A large, dark blue, almost black Chevy SUV traveled down Dans Run Road about two miles from the little town of Patterson Creek. It rounded a turn and in the distance, the driver noted a West Virginia State Police car blocking the side road that went to an old farmhouse. The blue lights on the patrol car came on and it pulled onto the main road, Dans Run Road, blocking it. The SUV slowed and stopped at a respectable distance. For what seemed like an eternity but was less than one-half a minute, the two vehicles faced each other. Then two box truck ambulances, one with Fort Ashby Volunteer Fire Department on the side and the other with Patterson Creek Volunteer Fire Department painted on the side, slowly rolled down the old farm road and turned right onto Dans Run Road. They headed toward the town of Patterson Creek in no hurry. The patrol car remained blocking the road with its blue lights still flashing. Soon a red fire truck from the Patterson Creek Vol. Fire Dept. came down the old farm road and also turned right as the two other emergency vehicles had. The patrol car remained blocking the road for a short time more. Then it backed up and blocked the lane to the farmhouse again. The officer in the car turned the lights off.

With this, the dark Chevy SUV continued its journey toward Patterson Creek. As the driver rounded the turn before the low water bridge over the creek, he noticed the fire truck parked on the gravel by the stream. The firemen had a hose from the truck ran to the water and were filling up the big tank of the fire truck.

The SUV stopped by the truck and the dark shaded electric window rolled down. A voice yelled out to the firemen by the truck, "Hey, Bob, how's it going? Long time no see."

Bob Bradshaw looked to the SUV, but could not see who was calling him. He walked to the window of the truck in his bulky fireman's gear. "Oh, hi, Mr. Godfrey. I'm doin' fine. How about you?"

"Oh, I've had better days, but I've had worse. I saw the ambulances and your fire truck come down from the old farm. What's happened? Did the old place burn down? Anybody hurt?" he asked.

"There was a shooting up there. Two guys shot each other for some reason. Kind of strange circumstances," he said.

"What do you mean?" the driver asked.

"I can't say much more. There's a police investigation going on. You can read all about it in the paper tomorrow," Bob replied.

The two men made a little more chitchat, said good-bye, and then the big SUV drove off.

The next day Mister Godfrey did read the report in the *Cumberland Times News*. He could tell the cub reporter had written his piece directly from information in a police report. *Journalism isn't what it use to be,* he thought. In the old days, the reporters always hunted out details that are always left out of the official report. And he knew important details were missing from this one. The details would surface eventually. He was sure of that.

* * * *

The Voice sat in his chair. In his hand was the police report of the double homicide that occurred at an old farmhouse near Patterson Creek. He read the account of the slayings from the local newspaper. Both reports lacked details as he knew they would. *Just what really had happened on his operation there?*

He needed to know. *Had his two men got into an argument and killed each other?* He knew there was more. The report had no mention of the marijuana grow house. He had people in his pocket that could get him the details if this had happened in Maryland, but he had little success penetrating the West Virginia government people. One man he had compromised had been brought down by his own greed and gone to jail. Another like to drive fast, too fast on the crooked WV roads in his muscle car. He and his wife were both killed while racing around on US 50 east on Romney near Gore just outside of Winchester. He knew the silence indicated the cops did not know who was behind it and would be going over things with a fine-tooth comb. He could see no way they could trace it back to him. The cheap phones the men carried from his organization were untraceable. He had been careful, but there was always the chance of a mistake. All plans had flaws. The ones you could see, you could deal with. Others could only be seen with "xrays." Still, others could remain hidden till they appeared with disastrous results. Perhaps this was one of them. Perhaps not, but of this one thing he was sure. He was disappointed, very disappointed and it was not good to disappoint the Voice.

Chapter 44

Tom at the hospital

Oooooh, my head hurts. Tom slowly opened his eyes. He looked around. *Where am I? This place looks like a hospital. What happened? Why am I here?* An IV was in his hand and he was lying in a clean bed with sterile, white sheets. Just then, a nurse came into the room. Tom spoke to her, "Nurse, what I am I doing here?"

She was surprised. "Just a minute, I get you a doctor," she said.

She quickly returned with a woman in a white doctor's clothing. "Hello, Mister Kenney. I'm Doctor Fletcher. You gave us quite a scare. Your wife is in the cafeteria eating. We are getting her. You're at the VA Hospital in Cumberland."

"Thought this place looks vaguely familiar," Tom said, "but what am I doing here?"

"Two days ago you were shot. A bullet grazed your skull. You are lucky to be alive," the doctor said.

Tom was startled. "I don't remember what happened," he said.

"We'll call the police and let them know you are conscious. They will explain everything. And I know they want to talk to you badly. A Sheriff Wagoner has been calling every other hour asking about your condition," the doctor said.

At that moment Tom's wife Joann came in the room. "Oh, Tom! We thought we'd lost you!" She cried as she hugged him.

"I love you too, honey." Tom replied. "What am I doing here?"

"You were shot with a pistol. The bullet creased your head. Down at Patterson Creek, at the old farm," she said.

Tom shook his head. "You really don't remember, do you?" Joann asked.

Again Tom shook his head.

"Okay," the doctor said. "We need to back up. Mr. Kenney, two days ago you were brought in here unconscious with a gunshot wound to your head. You have lapsed in and out of sleep and semi-consciousness. Besides the gunshot wound, you've had an acute stress reaction, probably related to the PTSD you have been treated for here in the past. Your wife has been here the whole time. She can tell you about it. And a big, black priest was here all day yesterday. He asked to be notified as soon as you regained consciousness. And a host of others did, too."

Tom smiled. He was so fortunate to have so many friends.

"Are you feeling okay?" asked the doctor.

Tom nodded yes.

"Good, I was worried about you," the doctor said. "I'll leave you two alone for a while. I'll check on you later." With that, she turned and was out the door along with the nurse who followed him.

"Oh, honey, I thought you might never awake. I love you," Joann cooed.

"I love you, too," Tom said. "What happened to me? I just don't remember."

"Sheriff Wagoner said he found you siting on the porch of an old house near Patterson Creek with blood running down your head from the bullet wound," she said. "When he asked you what happened, you pointed with your left hand to two dead men about one hundred feet away. You called Doug on your cell phone. All he could get out of you was 'help me' and 'Patterson Creek.' Lucky for us, you forgot to take that little map with directions there. Doug found it at your desk and called 911. The sheriff was at Linda's Restaurant when he got the call. He found you and the others about 10 minutes later. "

Tom said, "The last thing I remember was leaving the office. Everything from there to here is a big blank space."

"The doctor said with acute stress like you've had, you may never be able to fill in the blanks. You scared us. You were back fighting in Vietnam. You relived Sarah's death," she said. She lowered her eyes. "And Brian's."

Tom could say nothing. He had seen so much death in his life: friends in Vietnam, Sarah, his first wife, another victim of bloody Route 28. And Brian. It had been he who found Brian. Tom could feel all the pain again. *Oh God,* he thought, *is this how You felt when Your son died? How did you survive the pain? Oh God, how?*

"Tom," Joann said, "You kept repeating '**why**?' over and over."

Tom laid there and said nothing. *Why?* He wished he knew. The pain in his heart was far worse than the pain in his head.

At that moment a voice said, "I hate break this up, but I need to talk to you, Tom." Sheriff Wagoner said as he walked into the room.

"Sheriff, I'd offer you coffee, if I had some," Tom said. "Grab a chair."

"And donuts, can't forget the donuts," said the sheriff with a grin.

Joann looked at the sheriff. "Sheriff, when you two are done, let me know. I'll be waiting at the cafeteria." And with that she was gone.

The sheriff looked at Tom thoughtfully. "Tom, you scared the living heck out of me. I found you bleeding and in a daze."

"Acute stress reaction the doctor called it," Tom stated.

The sheriff started, "That's what he told me, too. He said you may never remember what happened or maybe just bits and pieces. Do you remember who shot you?"

Tom shook his head no.

"Why were you there at the farmhouse on the hill?" inquired the sheriff.

Tom shook his head. "I don't know. I can't remember."

"Who were the two dead men? the sheriff asked. "We are waiting for the results on finger prints."

Tom thought for a long minute. "You need to check out the names Alan Grey and Mike Levy. Those names seem familiar for some reason."

"We will and Tom, we know you had nothing to do with the killings." The sheriff continued, 'The crime scene guys checked your hands for gun power residues, nothing."

Tom breathed a sigh of relief.

"Do you remember anything else that might help us?" asked the sheriff.

"No, it's a big fat blank from the time I left the office two days ago till I woke up here."

"Well, thanks," said Sheriff Wagoner. "We'll see what comes up under those two names. If you remember anything more, even something small, and trivial, call us. It may be the clue we need to solve this. I've been a cop for a long time and this one has a really strange smell to it. You know what I mean?"

Tom nodded.

The sheriff got up to leave. "If you remember anything, call me immediately. Hey, gotta go. They're probably speeding out on Route 28, or hot rodding on Route 46. Don't forget, call me." The sheriff said this as he held his hand up like an open phone next to his ear. "Anything, call me."

Tom said he would and the sheriff left. Soon Joann reappeared.

"I called the Padre. He said he'd be here soon," Joann said.

Tom said he couldn't wait to see him, but by the time he got there, Tom was sound asleep, again.

The doctor told Joann and the Padre that it was not unusual. Acute stress will wear a body out quickly. And Tom would sleep another twenty-four hours straight before waking up.

Chapter 45

Tom awoke and it was still dark. He looked at the clock on the dresser. Soon it would be getting light. He eased out of bed so not to wake up Joann. It had been his best night's sleep since the shooting, almost two weeks ago now. In the kitchen, he put the coffee on to perk. He dressed quickly, poured the now ready coffee into an insulated bottle. *Chock Full o'Nuts, great coffee, nectar of the gods,* he thought. Tom wrote a quick note, "Honey, went to my thinking place," then very carefully and silently, walked out the back door. It was still dark, but Tom knew the way like the back of his hand.

From out of the darkness came Tom's two dogs, a Chow-German shepherd mix named Wolf and a beagle-something mix he called Gipper after Ronald Reagan. Tom felt he was the only good president he could remember. They were happy to see Tom. He shushed their barking. He didn't want them to wake the wife. Let her sleep. After giving them some water and dog chow, he told them to stay at the house, though he knew there was only a 50-50 chance they would listen. They loved to be with him. The dogs also were his nighttime security around the bottling facility. The beagle mix had the better hearing and usually alerted the two to anything needing investigating. The larger dog looked like he could tear your leg off, but actually was the friendlier of the two, but strangers didn't know that and didn't need to. He went around the bottling building. Next to the old barn stood Nacho, the donkey. He began braying loudly when he saw Tom. "Nacho!" Tom tried to yell quietly, "Be quiet!"

He continued to bray until Tom got to him and rubbed his head. "Quiet, Nacho. People are trying to sleep," said Tom.

Tom continued to scratch Nacho behind his ears. A satisfied noise came from the Jerusalem donkey's throat. He sure looked better now than when he came in. Tom could remember the call from Sheriff Donnie Wagoner. "Hey, Tom, I got a donkey here. I need to find a temporary place to keep him. We took him from a man who was neglecting him. He was cooped up in a shed with little to no food. I thought about putting him down. He's in bad shape, but maybe he can be saved. What do you say? Can you keep him till we can find a good home?"

Tom asked, "Same pay as last time?"

He could hear the shrug in Donnie's voice, "Yah, I'm afraid so."

Tom knew what that meant, same pay he received on the other animal rescues, nothing. "Yah, bring him over. I'll see if he's savable."

When the truck with the donkey arrived, Tom could see why Donnie considered putting him down. He was nothing but skin and bones. Tom gave the credit for the healthy animal that stood behind the fence to Miriah, Joann's daughter. She loved animals and had done the impossible with Nacho.

"Nacho, you be quiet. I got to go. I'll bring you some apples when I come back," said Tom. He scratched the donkey and walked up the old steep road. The donkey followed silently and stopped at the fence at the end of the pasture. There was no more braying. The road lead to the old hay field and orchard in the hollow area between two of the hilly knobs that helped give Knobley Mountain its name. The old road didn't get much use now. Some years ago when times were really tough, a group of people that like to hang glide paid him to use his property on the hill behind the house. Tom had watched them jump off the cliffs on the Maryland facing side. He thought they must be crazy, but they seemed to enjoy it.

"Come on," they said. "We'll show you how to do it."

Tom had politely refused. They usually soared over the Potomac and landed in a field by the river in Maryland. One day when conditions were right, he saw they were flying like birds, hundreds of feet above the top of Knobley.

He hiked up the road, now little more than two rutted paths. Tom made his way in the dim light upward. It was along this road he shot his first squirrel, one of the rites of passage into manhood for a county boy. He had bagged many bushy tails among the oak and hickory trees on this hill side. After ten minutes, he was at the old field and dawn was breaking. He loved this time of day and this place. It was his piece of almost heaven, West Virginia. A noise to his left started him. A deer ran by quickly. *I wonder what spooked him?* thought Tom.

He shot his first deer up here, a six-point buck. Soon his dogs appeared. They wagged their tails when they saw him, though he could tell they knew he had told them to stay at the house.

Nevertheless, Tom was happy to see them. He talked softly to them and petted their heads and backs. The dogs were happy for the approval of their master and licked his hands. He sat down on a log with his four legged companions. The sunrise was beautiful, but he knew that someone had tried to kill him two weeks ago and he still could not remember who or why. It was still a total blank from the time he left the office until he woke in the hospital. The bandaged wound on his head would leave a scar, a testimonial of what happened for Tom and all to see. *Would the memories come back?* He was not sure he wanted to know, but he had a feeling this was not the end of this matter. As Hans Solo in the *Star Wars* movie said, "I got a bad feeling about this."

Chapter 46

Tom had been up here many times to think. It was so peaceful here. The sun was now over the eastern horizon and bathed the mountaintop in light. With the arrival of cooler weather, the leaves were turning colors. The oaks were various shades of red, some crimson, some vermillion, and some fire engine red. Yellow and orange were added by the maples and poplars. The hills of West Virginia were being painted by the Master's hand. It was here in this meadow that Tom, after the deaths of Sarah and Brian had cried out, "Why?" to his Lord. It was here the still small voice spoke to him. "For such a time as this," It said. Tom still hurt, but he knew God had a plan, and God had not forgotten him. Just like Esther in ancient Persia, he was where he was supposed to be. Today Tom had come up for the solitude and to ask why again. *Why had someone wanted to kill him? Why was there so much suffering?* He almost wished he had been killed and was at peace with his son and wife. *Why Lord?* Someday it would all be clear, but now it was like looking through muddy water. And there were still holes in his recent memories besides the time of his getting shot. He sat on a fallen tree and pet the dogs. The beagle mix scratched at an itch, then got up and sniffed at something close by. Tom took a look at what he found. Scat, bear scat. Well, here was the answer to the question. Does a bear chip in the woods? Yes, indeedy—and it looked like he had been eating apples. It sure wasn't apple sauce after going through the bear. This reminded Tom of what became of his tax dollars. Put good stuff in one end and what do you get out the end? Nothin'.

More time passed as Tom continued to enjoy the quiet and aloneness on his mountain. The sun was now up higher and it was time to go. Tom grabbed some fallen apples for Nacho. He found one still hanging from the tree. Tom bit in and it was still good and tasty. An apple a day keeps the doctor away Mom had always said. He headed through the damp meadow to the old road down the hill. It was a lot quicker going down than coming up. Nacho was patiently waiting and Tom gave him the apples which he ate. He heard noise up the old road and here came the dogs. They ran toward the house. *Guess, it's breakfast time for all God's creatures including me,* Tom thought. *I'm hungry.*

Tom got the big bag of dog food out and fed the canines—they wolfed it down. Tom walked into the house and looked at the clock, 8:30 a.m. He put another pot of coffee on and grabbed the bag of muesli cereal and some milk for his breakfast. He found a note on the table from Joann. It said, "Call Sean Frazee ASAP, important."

Joann had left for Sunday school at the church. Tom wanted another week off before returning to church and work. Tom picked up the phone and called Sean's cell phone. Sean, pastor of Calvary Chapel Morgantown, was scheduled to lead the services this morning at Calvary Chapel Fort Ashby that met at the town Community Center. Sean's phone range twice—he picked it up. "Hello, this is Sean. Tom is that you?"

"Yes, it's me. What the emergency? You are still gonna make it today for services at 10:00 right?" Tom asked.

"That's what I needed to talk to you about. I've been sitting on the Cheat Lake Bridge on I 68 for the last forty-five minutes. A big rig lost its brakes coming down Chestnut Ridge and wrecked just before the bridge on the east side. The Interstate is closed and I'm stuck on the bridge. It's going to be several hours before traffic is moving again. Sorry Tom, there is no way I can make services at 10:00," Sean said. "I know you were counting on me, but I'm between a rock and a hard spot, well actually a Toyota and big rig. I really hate to let you down."

Tom said he was glad to hear Sean had not been involved in the accident and he would have to come up with something between now and service time. *What now, Lord?* thought Tom. *I know you say to be ready at all times to present the Good News, but I was hoping for another week of down time. Guess you had other plans. I do the services today, or it doesn't get done.*

The trip from his house to Fort Ashby was a blur to him. Tom still had not decided on what to teach. The people at the church were all glad to see Tom. He never believed he could be hugged so much and still survive. *What would he do without his church family, his friends?* At ten o'clock, services began with Mary Barrett singing and playing guitar. Tom had always loved her singing, but today her first three songs were a blur. And then they began to sing an old song, "My Jesus, I love thee" written by William R. Featherston in 1864.

My Jesus, I love thee, I know thou art mine.
For thee all the follies of sin I resign,
My gracious Redeemer, my Savior are thou:
If ever I loved thee, my Jesus, 'tis now.

The last line roused Tom, "If ever I loved Thee, my Jesus, 'tis now." *Where would I be without you Lord?* Tom thought, *You are my rock, my anchor.*

I love Thee because Thou hast first loved me,
And purchased my pardon on Calvary's tree;
I love thee for wearing the thorns on thy brow;
If ever I loved Thee, My Jesus 'tis now.

Thank you Lord, Tom thought, *for sacrificing yourself to pardon a mess like me.*
I'll love thee in life, I will love Thee in death,
And praise Thee as long as thou lendest me breath;
And say when the death dew lies cold on my brow,
If ever I loved Thee, my Jesus is now.

Tom now knew what God wanted him to speak on today.

In mansions of glory and endless delight,
I'll ever adore Thee in heaven so bright,
I'll sing with the glittering crown on my brow,
If ever I loved thee, my Jesus, 'tis now.

After this, Mary placed her faithful guitar in its upright holder and took a seat near the front. Tom got up from his seat and went to the front of the church. About forty pairs of eyes looked back at him. It was a good crowd today. Most of the smiling faces he knew. There were a few visitors and a classmate from high school Tom hadn't seen in a while and this was his first time here.

Tom said, "Good Morning."

The congregation responded, "Good morning."

Tom continued, "I wasn't expecting to be here this morning, but God had other plans. Our guest speaker, Sean Frazee of Calvary Chapel Morgantown is stuck in traffic out on Interstate 68 and won't be here. Most of you know I was taking some time off. I had an accident."

He pointed to the bandage on his head. "I got shot. A man tried to take my life about two weeks ago. I didn't know what I was to speak on till we sang the last song. The words, 'I'll love thee in life, I will love thee in life or death and praise Thee as long as thou lendest me breath' says it all. Psalms 144:4 says, 'Man is like a breath, His days are like a passing shadow.' Another place says, 'Man is but a vapor, gone by mid morn.' Life is very short and it can end at any time. Why God has me still here is a mystery to me. I could have died in Vietnam, many did. Several other times, I have felt death's cold breath on my neck. I could have died at a gunman's hand on a ridge near here. I still can't remember any of it, but I have this as proof it happened," and he pointed to the bandage on his head.

"David said in Psalms 138, 'I will praise you with my whole heart, before the gods, I will sing praises to you, I will worship toward your holy temple and praise Your name, for your loving kindness and your truth. You have magnified Your word above Your name. In the day I cried out, You answered me and made me bold with strength in my soul.'"

"Many of you here know how I lost my wife Sarah and my son Brian. I felt like Job. I knew his sorrows. But just like Job, I had to say, 'You are God and I am not.' As Solomon puts it in Ecclesiastes, 'There is a season for every purpose under heaven. A time to be born, a time to die; a time to plant, a time to harvest; a time to break down, a time to build up. A time to laugh and time to weep. A time of war, a time of peace.' And today it is time for some of you to give your lives to the Lord. This is not a time to hold back. This is the time, your time to say yes to Jesus. Yes, I need you as Savior and Lord. Yes, I can't live without you. I no longer want this life of sin. I want you as my King, Jesus. Come forward now and receive His forgiveness. Mary do you have a song?"

Mary got up and got her guitar and began:

"In moments like this, I sing out a song,
I sing out a love song to Jesus,
In moments like this, I lift up my hands.
I lift up my hands to the Lord.

Singing I live you Lord,
Singing I live you Lord.
Singing I love you Lord,
I love you."

And as she sang, Robert O'Brien, Tom's old classmate from high school came forward and gave his life to the Lord. In heaven, the angels danced for joy. And for Mr. O'Brien, the Irishman, they did a Holy jig unto the Lord, a celebration for a lost man come home.

Chapter 47

September 1985

It was a beautiful fall day in West Virginia. The temperature was near 70 degrees. William Kirkendall rode the old green and yellow John Deere tractor with its attached plow up the cow path toward the gate to the field on the grassy knoll high above Patterson Creek. His family had owned this farm for almost 200 years. At that time, he was unaware that earlier several miles away a man going to work in the darkness had crashed his car into the bridge on WV Route 46. The police had found the wrecked car, but not the driver who had disappeared. Unknown to them, hurt, bloody, and dazed he had stumbled from his car, fallen over the railing of the bridge, and drowned in the deep water below. Two weeks later, his bloated body would rise from the deep and float down the higher than normal waters of the creek. There had been a lot rainfall this year. His body would be found by two frightened children playing behind their house at the old dam near the VFW. The cops would put two and two together to solve the mystery of the missing man. But at that time, William knew none of this. He would read about it later in the newspaper. He did know it was a beautiful day to be a farmer. He had turned the farm near the 4H camp, Camp Minco, over to his son William, junior, who most people knew as Junior or just June. Thus had started a long line of William Kirkendalls. There were now four and William IV's young wife was pregnant. The old man wondered what they would name the child. *Another William? William V, maybe? It was up to them. Five generations of Kirkendalls all alive at the same time. What a family picture that would make. And men at that. But what if it's a girl? What if it's a girl? What would they name her? Willamina maybe? It was up to them. Boy or girl, old William could hardly wait for the new arrival. Susy was due around Christmas. What a Christmas gift that would be.*

William had enjoyed the life of a farmer, but it was tougher today. The old farm was now a second job for his son who drove a school bus for the county to supplement his income. The old man stopped the tractor, opened the gate, and drove in the grassy field overlooking the creek. Plowing up the field was his job today and he was glad to be able to do it. Two months ago, Dorothy, his wife of sixty-four years and the mother of his six children, five still living, had died peacefully in her sleep next to him. He had loved her till the end. The last two years had been hard, Alzheimer's disease. He had watched his loving, vibrant wife change into a sometimes vile, frail woman who forgot who he was and even to eat if not prompted. Someday he would ask the Lord why things like this happened. But now he knew she was at peace, no more suffering, no more pain. He had been her care giver to the end. Others, including his son, had advised him to put her in a nursing home, but he had vowed for better or worse. When she got nasty, he'd think *that's the Alzheimers talking. That's not my Dorothy.*

He knew the day may come when he could no longer care for her and he may need to do just that, but death had taken her before that. He held no hard feelings for those who had chosen differently. He knew first-hand how hard caring for her had been. Now she was at rest in the arms of Jesus and that gave him comfort.

He sat for a moment looking at the field. Through his slightly cataract clouded eyes, he make his plan of attack with the plow. When the cataracts matured a little more, he would have his eyes fixed at the clinic in Moundsville. He had given up driving on the highway, but felt comfortable on the tractor on familiar grounds. William had about five acres to turn over. The county agent had convinced Junior to switch his wheat crop over to a newer variety. The senior Kirkendall had urged his son to use caution. Plant a small area to see the county agent's advice was sound or not. Old Will remembered taking the advice of a long dead former agent on planting multiflora rose for living fence rows. It had worked well at first, but then the birds ate the red seeds, and carried them everywhere to sprout. It became a real fiasco. It had taken years, much money and effort to eradicate the noxious, invasive rose. Well-meaning people can still give bad advice. Old Will lowered the plow and began. Back and forth, forth and back he went again and again. The old field plowed easy, except for two lines about 100 feet apart by his estimates. There were parallel rock ridges here in the ridge and valley section of the Appalachians, but to his farm-trained mind the obstructions seemed more like roots, but in a line? That puzzled the old man. Still, he continued with his planned work. There were no more obstacles he could see in the field, except maybe for that little sycamore sapling in the middle of the field. He remembered that a monstrous giant of a tree had stood there years ago. What it had been doing growing up on the hill, he did not know. Sycamores are water loving trees and were normally found very close to water. Age and the ravages of nature had taken their toll on the old tree and now the only evidence of its long existence was a four-foot tall sapling sprouting from an old root that refused to die. He remembered when he and his granddad would sit at the foot of the huge tree and talk. William had learned much from his granddad. The old man knew much about the history of this area and its fauna and flora. He called the old tree a buttonwood because the pioneers made buttons from its workable wood. No one use that name anymore. And it would soon be gone, a victim of the John Deere's plow. William slowed as he approached the old tree's former location. There could still be some big, old roots from the tree there. Chunk! He'd hit something. It didn't sound like wood, but more like metal. He raised the plow from the soil. *What in blazes?* Through his cloudy eyes, he saw a dirty, rust-covered pipe about three feet long caught in his plow. He got off the machine and took a closer look at the catch. *Wonder who left this piece of junk here* he thought? He hopped back on the tractor and drove it over to the end of the field. There high above a near vertical shale cliff, he dislodged the unwanted item and rolled it to the edge. Even to his strong arms, the old rusty pipe was a challenge. It felt like it was full of lead. He pushed it over the edge and watched it roll down the steep slope. It went over several rare endangered indigenous plant species that only grow on the shale banks in this part of the world and through a patch of opuntia cactus sending pieces of the thorny pads flying, but William's clouded eyes missed these details. He saw the great splash as the fast moving, heavy object hit the water and disappeared into the deep, murky water where the creek made a horseshoe shaped curve. He finished plowing the field without further event, drove home through the cow pasture, and had a good supper his daughter-in-law had prepared for her work-weary men.

One month later, a tropical storm formed in the Gulf of Mexico. The erratic moving weather maker became Hurricane Juan. It made landfall in Louisiana, looped around, and again make landfall this time in the Florida panhandle. There was excessive rainfall, but minimal flooding in the southern states. In early November, the remnants of Hurricane Juan combined with a low-pressure system that stalled over the Appalachian Mountains. This moisture saturated system caused severe flooding in large areas of both Virginia and West Virginia, and significant flooding in smaller areas of neighboring Maryland and Pennsylvania. The good people of Fort Ashby described it as a storm of biblical proportions. Stream flow records were shattered throughout the affected areas. The flooding in West Virginia was the worst in the state's history. Fifty-two lives were lost. Numerous homes, outbuildings, roads, and bridges were destroyed. Damages were estimated at $578 million in West Virginia alone. The worst hit places were the Cheat River and South Branch of the Potomac valleys. And Patterson Creek flowed in a mountain valley between them. There the normally shallow and placid waters of the creek became a raging tiger. Two people were rescued from a house floating down the torrent by a helicopter. Huge trees a hundred years old were uprooted and swept away. Boulders the size of cars rolled like balls down the creek bed. And one old, rusty and forgotten swivel gun was caught up in the flood and swept away. And it was still full of gold, Braddock's Gold.

Excerpt from Jay Heavner's next book--

Hunter's Moon

The early morning night sky was crystal clear and the temperature was a cool, damp 45 degrees. The Hunter's Moon had been up all night shinning brightly, illuminating the Appalachian hills. In the old farm house he knew as home since childhood, Tom Kenney tossed and turned the night away. This was far from the first time this had happened, but tonight was different. Usually the nightmares were from the Post Traumatic Stress Disorder the ex-Army man experienced from the horrible battle at Ia Drang, Vietnam. Many brave, young men on both sides died there in the days of the battle. Nor were the night terrors from the tragic death of his first wife, Sarah, in the auto accident caused by the drunk driver. Nor was it about the suicide of his older son, Brian. He took his life on the one year anniversary of his mother's death over five years ago. The strain of this sent the young man suffering from schizophrenia over the edge. No, tonight it was different. A new fear ran wild through Tom's troubled mind. The incident that happened a month ago gnawed inside his head. *Why did they let him live? Why didn't they kill him? Why?*

Tom had been in and out of sleep the whole night. He rolled on his right side and looked at the bright red numbers on the small clock on the dresser, 04:15. *How many times had he looked at that clock tonight?* He rolled over onto his back and lay there staring at the high ceiling of the old house. Joann, his second wife, lay sleeping next to him. She had a head cold and hadn't been feeling well. The stopped-up nose caused her to snore most of the night. Normally, this would have bothered Tom, but tonight the rhythmic noise had been a comfort. He needed someone there, even a snoring, sick, sleeping wife. The light from the Hunter's Moon peeked around the curtain at the window in the dark bedroom. Tom was now wide awake and he knew there would be no more sleep for him tonight. He got out of bed and walked to the window. He pulled the curtain aside and looked at the mountain—his mountain, bathed in moonlight. It called to something inside of him and he knew he must answer. Many times in his life he found comfort among the rocks and trees there. And today would be no different.

He felt the window pane and found it cool. He would need a jacket to fight off the chill this morn. Quickly he dressed and headed for the kitchen. He grabbed two apples, two granola bars, and put a cup of hot water in a paper cup in the microwave oven for one minute. Today he would have instant coffee. He was in a hurry. He needed his mountain. The bell on the microwave dinged and he took out the steaming hot cup, sat it on the counter, and poured the coffee crystals into the cup. Slowly he stirred the dark liquid, and took a refreshing sip. It was then he heard the floor board behind him creak. He turned with a start. Five feet away from him stood his young stepdaughter Miriah rubbing her sleepy eyes. She had an old rag monkey doll under her arm. "What wrong, Daddy? Bad dreams again?"

Tom sat the coffee down on the counter and went over to her. He picked her up in his strong arms and tenderly said to her, "Yes, bad dreams again, honey, bad dreams."

She hugged him back, and smiled to him. "We can't have that." She bowed her little head that was covered in long wavy brown hair and prayed, "Dear Jesus, help my daddy. Chase the bad dreams away. Amen."

"Amen," repeated Tom. Though Tom was her step dad, she loved him like a father, and Tom loved her, too. She had become the daughter he always wanted. His first wife, Sarah and he, had only boys. "Now," he said as he put her down, "you get back to bed and tell Mommy I went up on the mountain."

She nodded her little head, turned, and started out of the kitchen, but stopped. She turned, smiled, and said, "Love you, Daddy."

Tom responded, "And I love you, too, little darlin'."

She turned again and disappeared out of the kitchen. That young lady had Tom wrapped around her little finger. He knew it and didn't care. Right now he needed all the encouragement and love available. He took a piece of note paper and wrote a quick line to Joann telling her of his intent to go up on his mountain. He put it on the counter and headed towards the back door. Carefully he opened the door, stepped outside, and closed it making a minimum of noise. He did not want to waken his sleeping wife, nor any other member of the family. As he walked away, he heard a questioning and challenging "woof" behind him. "Tripod," he whispered. "It's me."

With that Tripod let out a satisfied 'woof', hopped up to him on his three good legs, and did a little dance around Tom's feet. "Tripod, be quiet. People are trying to sleep."

The dog looked at him knowingly and put his muzzle in Tom's waiting hands. Tom rubbed the happy dog around his furry head, much to the dog's delight. Tripod had replaced one of Tom's two dogs that got sick and died recently. Miriah found him more dead than alive lying in a ditch along the main road on her way home from school one day. He had been hit by a car and had a mangled rear leg. They took him to the county veterinarian who advised them to put the injured dog down, but Miriah pleaded for his life. Tom told the dog doctor to do what he could and to everyone's surprise, except Miriah's, the dog lived and recovered quickly. She just had a way with animals.

Tom started up toward the bottled water warehouse behind the farm house with the dog following on all fours, well, all threes as was the case. Tom looked at the happy dog. "Okay, Tripod, you can come along." He seemed to let out a knowing "woof."

Tom looked at the three legged dog. He seemed to be content just as he was and did not seem to note his missing leg. Tom knew there was a lesson standing with him, but he was in no mood for a lesson right now.

The events of that recent painful day crept back into his mind. *Why, why did they let him live? Why didn't they kill him? They told him they would He knew they would. Why?*

The man and dog walked up to the old barn where Nacho, the Jerusalem donkey, called home. He was there standing next to Eor, the little burro rescued from a passing, traveling circus by the sheriff. She had been abused and was sick when the truck carrying her arrived at Tom's zoo as Miriah called the barn. She worked her loving magic on the little beast who slowly recovered.

The two members of the horse family walked over to the fence by the road going up the hollow and through the gap to the big field that sat high between the knobs on this segment of Knobley Mountain.

"Quiet, you two," said Tom. "I got something for you."

Their ears perked up, and Tom pulled the two apples from his coat pocket and gave one each to the eager animals. They ate them quickly. Tom rubbed their heads and necks which calmed them. They dropped their heads and began to graze on the weeds along the old farm road. Tom turned from the animals and with Tripod following, headed up the rutted two lane path. The Hunter's Moon was very bright, allowing Tom to navigate the road which he knew like the back of his hand without a flashlight. The trees still clung to their multicolored autumn leaves. The moonlight filtered through them. Progress was slow up the steep road and Tom was in no hurry. He needed to think and the walk on his mountain brought some peace to Tom's troubled soul.

Tripod, now ahead of him, stopped, sniffed the ground, and let out a snort through his nose. Tom looked at what had the dog's attention. There were tracks in the soft dirt in the road, large tracks that Tom thought must have come from a very large dog, but in the darkness, it was hard to tell. They continued up the road and the dog stopped again to sniff at something. Tom bent down to see what the dog had found. Scat. This was not from a large dog, but from a bear. Tom heard recent stories of bears returning to the local woods, but this was his first for sure conformation. If there was any question what a bear does in the woods, Tom had undeniable proof.

The first hint of daylight appeared above Middle Ridge on the eastern horizon. The lesser light, the Hunter's Moon, would soon be disappearing behind the imposing land mass known as Allegheny Front, that rose to form the western horizon. Between Tom's location and the front was the North Branch of the Potomac River and river valley. Soon the sun would bath the hills with light and the brilliant fall colors of the trees would shine. No place on earth had the variety of tree species to produce the kaleidoscope of colors found here in the Appalachian Mountains. The summer had been somewhat dry, but recent soaking rains provided more than adequate moisture for the intense annual display.

After the inspection of the bruin's droppings, Tom and his three legged companion continued up the old mountain road. The first rays of the sun were peeking over the eastern hills. Soon the majesty of the Creator's hand would be fully visible. Tom reached the high gap between two of the many knobs of Knobley Mountain. To anyone else the knobs may have all looked the same, but not to Tom. This was his mountain. This was home. He stopped and looked around. To the east, Patterson Creek Ridge rose like a dinosaur back among the many hills. To the west, the sun's long rays landed on Dan's Rock, high on the top edge of the front. The colors were incredible. The maples were a bright orange. The oak's colors varied by species. They ranged from scarlet and red to dark orange. Hickories showed a hue of yellows. Here and there the fall colors were broken by the dark greens of several kinds of pine. Tom came up here to be refreshed in this open air cathedral and it was working. He took a seat on the large flat rock, pulled a granola bar from his pocket, and began to eat it. He offered some to the dog, but he was not interested in the crunchy, sweet bar. Tom pulled a plastic half-liter bottle of water, Knobley Mountain Spring Water of course, from his hip pocket and took a long drink. His companion hydrated himself earlier from the small spring in the gap.

Tom's mind drifted off to the new incident that led to his nearly sleepless night.

It started out as just another day, nothing special, just another day. He had taken the truck into Cumberland to make deliveries in the downtown area. His last stop was the Cumberland Times News office. He backed the truck into the deliveries area, unloaded the large order and brought it into the building. A clerk counted the order for accuracy and signed off. Tom then distributed the 5 gallon bottles and 1/2 liter cases throughout the four story building. Everything was routine until he got to the long corridor that led outside in the lower level. The lights went off and he was plunged into total darkness. He had heard a door open, footsteps approaching, and then a blow to the head knocked him unconscious.

Sometime later, he awoke and found himself strapped soundly in a chair. Groggy, he looked around —the room was black—except for a single spotlight above him. He was an island of light in a sea of night darkness. He noted an IV in his strapped–tight, right hand. A tube led to a fluid bag suspended from a pole, tied to the chair that confined him. Tom felt no pain. From this fact, he knew the fluid going into his vein contained a sedative, a strong one, but strangely, his mind was remarkable clear.

Off to the right he heard a door open in the darkness. Two men walked in front of him. They were dressed in dark pants, white shirts, lab coats, and their heads were covered with white cloth sacks with crude eye holes cut in them.

The shorter man spoke, "Good day, Mr. Kenney. I trust you are comfortable." The voice was eerie and computer enhanced. It sent chills down Tom's back.

"Who are you and what do you want?" asked Tom.

"Direct and to the point," the enhanced voice spoke. "I like that quality in a man."

"Who are you and what do you want?' Tom asked again.

"Why, I am your Benefactor and you will provide me with information that I want," replied the modified voice.

"What information is that?" Tom continued.

"Braddock's Gold. You know where it is and I want that information. You were there at the farm on Patterson Creek when the two men died. You were there. You know where it is."

Tom smiled, "Yah, I was there, or so they tell me. I can't remember a thing that happened after I left my office that day. It's locked in my head if it really is there. I've been fighting Post Traumatic Stress Disorder since I was a soldier in Vietnam. It'll bury stuff in your mind and you can't remember."

The short man stiffened and he pointed his finger at Tom. "You will give us the information or you will die. My assistant here has a lethal dose of morphine waiting for you if we don't get that information."

"I don't know. It's just not there," pleaded Tom.

The short man paused for a moment and spoke to Tom, "Then you will die." He nodded knowingly to the big man next to him who said nothing. The big man stuck the syringe in the IV and injected a clear fluid slowly.

"I really don't know, I really don't know," he pleaded more.

Soon the clear fluid took effect and Tom lost consciousness.

The next thing he remembered was wakening up in the hospital with Joann sitting beside his bed. He was alive.

Why didn't they kill him? Why did they let him live? He couldn't stop them. Why?